Manxmouse

Manxmouse

Paul Gallico

text illustrations by Janet and Anne Grahame-Johnstone
cover illustration by Sumiko Davies

Piccolo
Pan Books in association with **William Heinemann**

First published 1968 by William Heinemann Ltd
This edition published 1972 by Pan Books Ltd,
Cavaye Place, London SW10 9PG,
in association with William Heinemann Ltd
2nd printing 1976
© Paul Gallico 1968
© A. G. Mathemata Anstalt 1968
Illustrations © William Heinemann Ltd 1968
ISBN 0 330 23379 3
Printed and bound in Great Britain by
Cox & Wyman Ltd, London, Reading and Fakenham

For Grace

Contents

Chapter   page

1   The Story of the Tiddly Mouse-Maker   9
2   The Story of Manxmouse and the Clutterbumph   23
3   The Story of the Happenings in Nasty   32
4   The Story of Manxmouse and Pilot Captain Hawk   41
5   The Story of the Great Bumbleton Mouse Hunt   54
6   The Story of Nervous Nelly   70
7   The Story of Wendy H. Troy   88
8   The Story of the Terrified Tiger   102
9   The Story of the Greedy Pet Shop Proprietor   120
10   The Story of the Marvellous Manx Mouse Auction   136
11   The Story of Manxmouse meets Manxmouse   151
12   The Story of Manxmouse meets Manx Cat   164

1

The Story of the Tiddly Mouse-Maker

THERE was once rather an extraordinary old ceramist who lived in the village of Buntingdowndale in the heart of England. Ceramics is the art of making pottery into tiles, or dishes, or small glazed figures.

What was unusual about him was that he only made mice. And they were not the ordinary kind either. Other potters in the village, and there were several, turned out birds or dogs, kittens or rabbits and many different kinds of animal, but this one made nothing but the most life-like and enchanting little ceramic mice from morning until night.

He was a happy fellow who hummed to himself contentedly throughout the day as, with his clever fingers, he modelled mouse after mouse after mouse. In the evening he would put those that were dry into a special oven and let them bake overnight. Then the next day he would take them out, polish them, file off the rough edges and look at them lovingly before either setting them in the window of his shop in Buntingdowndale or sending them off up to London.

He probably knew more about mice and their ways than anyone else in the world, so that he was able almost to think like a mouse.

He had come to know them so well because he had mice in his workshop—not in a cage of course, but whole families of them who lived there behind the wainscoting and underneath the wooden floor.

They were quite used to him and since he did not keep a cat, they would come out from their homes and go about their business across the room, or sit up to have a chat together as though he were not there. Sometimes he felt he could almost understand what they were saying. Thus he came to have a great affection for them, copying them in all kinds of poses. He made them as he saw them, coloured brown, grey or white, but their ears were always of a delicate pink and nearly transparent.

But just because he was so fond of them and so knowledgeable, he was never wholly satisfied with the results of his work. Something he felt each time escaped him— some attitude of the body, or expression of their faces. Oh, he made them look worried all right, since he knew that no sensible mouse ever relaxed entirely, even when there was no cat in the house. For there were other things to upset them; terriers, birds of prey, not to mention stoats, weazels and foxes. Then there were

10

traps set by people, and the everyday business of seeking out a living for their families and themselves.

And so the old gentleman's mice always seemed to be peering slightly nervously over their shoulders. Yet he felt that there was something about mousedom that he had failed to capture. But every time he set about his work, he was hoping that this next one would result in the absolutely faultless or super mouse.

So the days passed; people came from far and near to buy his figures, for they thought them perfect. But the ceramist was beginning to wonder whether before it came his time to pass on, he would ever be able to make a completely one-hundred-per-cent, satisfying reproduction.

And then, out of the blue, something happened. Sometimes when one has had an ambition for a lifetime, worked hard and tried faithfully, one can brew up a magic moment when suddenly all things seem possible. It was not exactly like that with this potter. The strange thing was that the feeling came to him on a day when he had not planned to do any work at all. For there was to be an important wedding of the daughter of friends in Buntingdowndale, and of course he had been invited.

It turned out to be a very happy and gay affair indeed, lasting all day. Beginning with the marriage in the morning there was a large luncheon with many toasts in cider drunk to the bride and groom. After the happy pair had left it was far too early to go home, so the potter with several of his cronies went to the village inn, The Cat and Mouse. He was particularly welcome there, for he had modelled the sign that hung over the door, in which the mouse was as large as the cat and the two were marching hand-in-hand and smiling cheerfully at one another. This idea, naturally, was quite absurd but it was so amusing and charmingly done that it had resulted in making the inn rather famous.

There, without regard to the clock, or the call of other duties, the friends continued to raise their glasses to the health and future happiness of the married couple, until to their great surprise the inn-keeper was compelled to announce closing time. Thereupon they rose and departed, each to his home in his own manner, with the ceramist finding it easier to float than to walk.

For he was feeling as though he weighed almost nothing, and he was exceptionally happy, joyful and contented.

The village street by lamplight had never looked more beautiful, nor the stars above brighter and it seemed to him that if he wished he could reach up and touch the moon. Some kind of enchantment was at work.

As he turned into the gate of his cottage he thought it was a pity to put such a feeling to bed and to sleep. And so instead of entering the door, he turned off and drifted down the path to his workshop which was at the bottom of the garden. There he switched on the lamps and, light as a feather, settled down at his pottery bench by the bins of different kinds and grades of clay that he used. Before his eyes swam his jars of paints and glazes in all hues, his brushes and his modelling knives. At the far end his electric oven with its knobs, switches and levers appeared to form itself into a face and figure with arms outstretched in invitation.

And thereupon the sensation came over him most intensely and the idea smote him like a stroke of lightning: *Now! Now, this very moment, here tonight, this instant, I shall make my super mouse.*

At last, at last! Everything that he ever seemed to have known both about mice and the making of glazed ceramic figures, came together. And at that particular instant he felt he was the greatest ceramist the world had ever known, and that the mouse that he was about to make would be the most beautiful and perfect that anyone had ever seen.

His coat apparently removed itself without his aid. When he slipped the string of his potter's apron over his head, it tied itself around his waist. And since his feet no longer needed to touch the ground, it was no effort at all for him to move quickly about his workshop.

He decided to use his favourite mixture—two parts of Copenhagen clay which he imported from Denmark, combined with one part from the banks of the Deedle, the brook that meandered through Buntingdowndale. This he moistened and worked together into a ball. Never had this part of the work gone so well.

With a singing in his heart he reflected upon what a wonderful artist he was and with the picture of this mouse in his mind, he began to model.

It was a sitting-up one upon which he had decided. It would be perched on its hindlegs with its two tiny paws held in front of its breast, clutching the end of its tail which would come winding out from beneath it, up around its side and over one arm.

That night his fingers were so thin and sensitive that he did not need any of his modelling knives, not even to etch the fine whiskers sprouting from its cheeks. For these he used his thumbnail. He was particularly proud of the ears. He knew that when glazed and fired, one would be able almost to see right through them, as he could see

through the ears of the live ones who came to visit him.

'What is art?' he said to himself, and then answered, 'Art is creation and I am a creator'. And he felt even better and happier.

It was the same with the preparation for the painting and glazing. He had only to think about what he wanted and there it was. All his skill, knowledge, cunning and experience were brought into play here. One had to know exactly the right mixture of colours, so that when the clay emerged from the furnace, the heat would have baked it into exactly the proper shades.

This was to be a dark grey mouse when it was finished. He applied the paints lovingly and with care. The tiny upstanding ears would be grey outside and their shells the faintest shade of pink, the colour of the very beginning of dawn. The tail was like the coat, dark grey at the base and growing lighter as it climbed up around the side of the mouse, until it disappeared into the paws of the little animal. The very end was hardly any colour at all, which was a most artistic and lifelike achievement. For, as everyone knows, there is no hair at the tip of a mouse's tail and this is very difficult to copy. Yet for the ceramist that evening, nothing was impossible.

But this was not all that he felt he was accomplishing, merely the making of a purely physical copy of one of his little grey friends from behind the wainscoting. Oh no! On this very special and extraordinary occasion the ceramist felt that he had hit upon the secret of why his other creations had been failures in his own

15

estimation, and this one was to be a success. It was because he had applied himself too much to the form and not sufficiently to the spirit. And so, concentrating most tremendously upon this master mouse, he tried to instil all the wisdom and knowledge that he himself had accumulated during his lifetime: mouse knowledge, people knowledge, things knowledge.

Of course, although the ceramist knew a great many facts, there was also a good deal he did not, since it is not possible to know everything. But this did not worry him. He was pouring all of himself that there was into the little creature that was so smoothly and beautifully taking shape beneath his fingers.

At last it was finished. He placed his creation upon an already baked tile and stood back to contemplate his handiwork. He could hardly bear to lock it up inside the oven and tear himself away from it. And yet if he wished to see it in its utmost perfection the next morning, delicately coloured and exquisitely glazed, he must of necessity do so.

'I am indeed a great artist,' he murmured, highly pleased with himself. He gently lifted up the tile which bore his sculpture and placed it in exactly the right position in the centre of the electric furnace, so that the heat would reach it evenly from all sides.

'Bake well, my little fellow,' he said, 'and tomorrow you will be a masterpiece.'

With this he examined the instruments to see that the temperature was rising properly and the thermostat working, and then, forgetting to switch off the lights in his workshop, he went out into the garden where he performed an impromptu dance of joy in celebration of his accomplishment. It was a good thing that it was late and the neighbours all abed, for they would have been most astounded had they seen the elderly, bespectacled ceramist leaping and pirouetting about upon the lawn.

When he had finished, he swam up the garden to his house. True, there was no water there, the night still being fine and dry, but at that moment he felt it would be lovely to swim along the path, through the cool grass. And so he did so, around and past his shop into his adjoining home, breast stroking his way up the stairs and right inside his bed, where no sooner did his head touch the pillow than he was instantly asleep. He dreamt that a gold medal was being handed him for creating the finest porcelain mouse ever.

When he awoke the next morning he was not feeling at all as well as he had upon retiring. Far from being able to float, he now seemed anchored to the bed because his head weighed as much as though it were made of lead. He had to put one foot at a time onto the floor and then saw to his amazement that he had not removed his clothes the night before. He wondered whether perhaps he was gravely ill. But then he remembered the wedding and the many glasses of cider that had been lifted, and the continuation of the party afterwards with his chums at The Cat and Mouse. What had occurred after that he did not recollect at all. He splashed cold water on his face, which did not help a great deal, and after drinking a number of cups of coffee, tottered off to his workshop.

To his astonishment he saw the light burning inside and his first thought was, *Burglars!*

He found the door unlocked which gave him further cause for alarm, and he hurried in to where another surprise awaited him. He observed that his electric oven was turned on to top heat, which was puzzling since he knew he had done no work the day before, but had attended a marriage instead.

Suddenly it began to come back to him, and he murmured, 'But of course, now I remember! Last night when I came home I made the most beautiful and the finest mouse of my whole life. Now I shall look at him.'

He switched off the oven and when it had cooled sufficiently, threw open the door. With hands that trembled slightly, he seized his pair of tongs and carefully withdrew the supposed mouse masterpiece from the depths of the stove and set it upon his workbench.

And then, with his eyes almost popping from his head and the most terrible sinking feeling in the pit of his stomach, he saw that what he had produced was not only no super creature, but a disaster second to none in the history of ceramics.

In the first place, it was not grey but an utterly mad blue. It had a fat little body like an opossum, hind feet like those of a kangaroo, the front paws of a monkey and instead of delicate and transparent ears, these were long and much like those of a rabbit. And what is more, they were blue too, and violently orange-coloured on the inside.

But the worst thing of all was that it had no tail. The ceramist examined the mouse from every angle and there was none to be seen, although at the back was a small button where one once might have begun. He had either forgotten to make it, or even more horrible thought, had been careless in its production and it had broken off.

Goodness knows, it didn't look like much of a mouse, what with no tail and rabbit's ears and wild blue in colour, but still it *felt* like a mouse and in some curious way was one. But, of course, as a ceramic it was a total failure.

And suddenly the artist threw back his head and began to roar with laughter as he said to himself, 'Well, I must have had a fine night. After coming here I can't remember a thing. Certainly no one ought to set about making porcelain mice, or anything else, when one has had several ciders over the eight.'

Now he examined the muddle of his clay and colourings and chemicals on the workbench and laughed even louder. He had used all the wrong materials and colours and had apparently just pulled any old chemicals off the shelf. And, of course, worst of all, he had not waited for it to dry before painting, glazing and baking. It was a wonder that anything at all had resulted from the mess.

One thing was certain, it was not the kind of product that a self-respecting ceramist would want to keep about his studio in case anyone should embarrass him by asking what it was. And so he raised a wooden mallet and was about to bring it down to smash it into dust, when something about the expression of the little creature caused him to stop.

To his surprise he found that the look on the face of the so-called mouse was peculiarly unusual and endearing.

The worry, the fear, the timorousness and feeling of wanting to glance over its shoulder to see whether the cat was around was missing. None of that. What it did have was a combination of interest and excitement with a little shyness and a great deal of sweetness.

If you looked at him from one angle, his face seemed to say, 'I love you! Please like me.' And from another, its expression was, 'I'm such a small mouse, I really don't matter to anyone. But I'd be happy to help you in any way I could.'

The ceramist laid down his mallet and picked up the porcelain piece which was now cool, and the gentleness and *differentness* of its face made him smile. Turning it around to the place where its tail should have been, he examined the button and then said, 'Oh well, so I've made a Manx Mouse.'

He was referring to the fact that the creature had no tail like the cats from the Isle of Man who, as everybody knows, are tail-less too, and are known as Manx Cats.

The figure looked so absurd that he was forced to smile again. 'Then I'll keep you to remind me to say "No thank you" next time I'm invited to have just one more glass.'

In the evening he took the Manx Mouse to his room and put it upon his bedside table where it sat up and re-garded him with a mixture of longing and affection, until he put out the light.

Now a strange thing occurred that night, so odd that when the ceramist told it to one of his chums he swore that he had imbibed nothing stronger than a glass of lime and barley water before retiring. For he was not aware that in spite of the weird results, cider or no cider, all the love and hopes he had poured into the making of this one mouse had called forth the magic of a true creation. And when that has taken place, anything can happen.

Thus it was that he woke up in the dark, or thought he did, with the feeling that the chiming clock in the living-room downstairs was about to strike, which indeed it did. He counted the strokes to know the time and how much longer there was left to sleep. And so he counted: eight, nine, ten, eleven, twelve, *thirteen*.

Thirteen! But that was absurd. No clock ever struck thirteen, and particularly not his faithful grandfather piece which had been in his family for years.

He had half a mind to get up and go downstairs and see what time it really was, but suddenly found himself drowsy and unable to keep his eyes open any more.

The following morning when he awoke, something even stranger had happened to occupy his attention. The Manx Mouse was no longer on his night table.

At first he thought that he must have knocked it off and so he looked on the floor and even crawled under the bed. But there was nothing there. Then he thought that perhaps it had got mixed up with the bedclothes, so he shook these out most carefully. But there was no Manx Mouse.

He then remembered vaguely what must have been a dream of the clock striking thirteen. This and the disappearance of the blue Manx Mouse was, to say the least, disquieting. He searched his room, looking in every nook and cranny and even in cupboards, bureau drawers and on top of shelves until there was not an inch that he had not inspected. In great perplexity he sat down on the edge of his bed and did not know what to think or where it could have gone, but finally had to give up.

And thus, having played his part, the ceramist now vanishes from our story.

But for Manxmouse, the adventure had just begun.

2

The Story of Manxmouse
and the Clutterbumph

IT was shortly after the stroke of thirteen
that Manxmouse realized that he was
sitting up on a night table next to a bed, where
a mouse really had no business to be.

The moonlight was pouring in through the
window, making a pathway to the door which was open.

There was a man asleep in the bed and he was snoring.
But he might wake up at any moment and Manxmouse
thought he had better go. He slid down one leg of the
table quite handily and slipped over to the side of the
room for a bit of shadow to think things over for a moment. For although he was certain that he ought to be
going, he did not know where to.

It was a most curious feeling not to have been aware of
being anywhere a few instants before and then quite
suddenly to be not only somewhere, but someone.
Perhaps that was what it was like to be born.

From the general shape of things he seemed to be a
mouse and indeed, he felt like a mouse and so he must
be one. But for the rest, how he had got on to a night table
and who, and what, and where he had been when he was

not anything or anybody, or even any place for that matter, was too difficult to understand. He did not even know his name, or if he had one. Thinking about it was beginning to give him a headache. If he was going to be on his way, now was the time to do it, before somebody came and shut the door.

He then did a very unmouselike thing. Instead of keeping to the shadows at the side of the room, he marched straight along the lighted path laid down by the moon across the carpet, to the door, climbed up the newel post at the top of the stairs and slid down the banisters. He got out of the front door and into the street through the letter-box.

Every single soul in Buntingdowndale must have been asleep. Except for a street lamp not a light showed anywhere. No one was about and even the houses had their eyes shut with blinds or curtains drawn.

There was a slight breeze blowing, bearing the scent of distant flowers and dew on grass. He thought he would be more comfortable in the country than in the midst of this brick, stone and glass. However, no sooner had he started off when, without warning, he encountered a Clutterbumph on the prowl through the village. It was looking for someone to entertain with a bad dream or a little agreeable terror in the night.

This was somewhat unusual, since it takes two to make a proper Clutterbumph.

For a Clutterbumph is something that is not there until one imagines it. And as it is always someone different who will be doing the imagining, no two Clutterbumphs are ever exactly alike. Whatever it is that frightens one the most and which is just about the worst thing one can think of, that is what a Clutterbumph looks like.

The Clutterbumph usually announces itself with a noise somewhere in the house during the night; a creak in a floorboard or a piece of furniture as it cools after the heat of the day, a drip from a tap, the rattle of a loose shutter, a fly buzzing on a windowpane, something scurrying in the attic, or a cricket caught in the coal cellar.

One could conjure up something with a sheet over it and two eye-holes, sitting on the end of the bed, or an ugly witch with a tall hat and hooked nose on a broomstick. Or perhaps one could imagine something that has too many legs and stingers fore and aft, or a great bear with fiery eyes and long claws and teeth. Or make it a one-eyed, snaggle-toothed giant nineteen feet tall, a dragon, a devil with a pitchfork, or just two googly eyes that keep staring.

The point is that the Clutterbumph cannot exist to frighten anyone unless that somebody thinks of it first and decides what it is going to be like. And when one has finished enjoying being frightened and does not want to be any longer, one simply stops thinking of the Clutterbumph, or falls asleep and it is not there any more.

Since Manxmouse was not imagining anything at the time, this particular Clutterbumph was as yet without any shape or form. In fact it was invisible and in its approach to Manxmouse it had to limit itself to such noises as,

'Whoooooooo!' and 'Ha!' and 'Grrrrr!' and also, 'Ho, ho, ho!' along with 'Boo!' or 'Shoo!' which last are rather old-fashioned and do not frighten anyone any more.

Although Manxmouse could see no one he thought he heard somebody speak and so he said, 'Good evening,' politely.

The Clutterbumph let out a screech 'Whoooeeeeeee! Good evening, indeed! We'll see about how good an evening it is.' And at this it snarled, growled, howled and roared. It stopped suddenly and in a more natural voice inquired, 'Look here, aren't you afraid?'

'I don't think so,' said Manxmouse.

'Oh, I say,' said the Clutterbumph in slightly injured tones, 'that's not playing the game. You're bound to be frightened of something: witches, ghosts, demons, dragons, monsters plain or fancy. I'm not particular and I'll be glad to oblige. Just think what it is that scares you the most and then I'll be with you in a jiffy. Perhaps I haven't introduced myself. I'm a Clutterbumph.'

Manxmouse genuinely wished to oblige the Clutterbumph, whatever it was, but found himself unable to do so. He said, 'I'm sorry, I really can't think of anything I'm frightened of.'

'Come, come!' said the voice, 'That's ridiculous. Not scared? What about dark corners when you never know what's going to jump out at you? That's something I do beautifully, by the way. I was first in my class jumping out from dark corners.'

'Please excuse me,' Manxmouse apologized, 'but you see, I haven't been here for very long and perhaps don't know how.' Which was quite true, since the ceramist had forgotten to put fear into him.

The Clutterbumph tried a different tack. He said, 'Let's be sensible. You're a mouse, aren't you?'

'I think so,' said Manxmouse.

'Well then,' cried the Clutterbumph triumphantly, 'you ought to be afraid of Cat. Ha! Wait till you see the kind of cat I can be. Made the Honour Roll for it—glowing eyes, cruel claws, sharp teeth, lashing tail and frightful growl. How about that?'

'But I've never seen a cat,' Manxmouse said.

'You're not being at all co-operative,' and a plaintive note crept into the voice of the Clutterbumph. 'Here I am, out on a job, one of the best of us, if I may say so—graduated with honours, with a gold medal for my appearance as a bogey, and I can't take shape and get on with my work unless you imagine me. Come on, now, there's a good mouse. Think up something simply awful.'

Manxmouse obviously wished to help and tried very hard, but nothing would come since, as he had already told the Clutterbumph, he had not been there for very long. And the truth is that no one is ever *born* frightened or fearing anything.

At last, after a period of awkward silence, the Clutterbumph moaned, 'All right, I give up. Forget about it. I've never been so humiliated in my life. What will they say back at the office, when they find out? A Clutterbumph who couldn't frighten a mouse! Oh dear, oh dear!'

'Do forgive me,' said Manxmouse.

The mouse was so plainly distressed, that the Clutterbumph said, 'That's all right. I shan't hold it against you. But if you wouldn't mind me giving you a little piece of advice . . .'

'Oh no, not at all,' said Manxmouse. 'It would be very kind of you.'

'Well,' said the Clutterbumph, 'I see you're a Manx Mouse.'

Since the Clutterbumph was invisible and, in fact, actually wasn't there, it was difficult to understand how he could 'see' anything. Nevertheless, Manxmouse replied, 'Am I?'

'Oh yes, undoubtedly. Anyone with half an eye, or even with no eyes like myself can see that. Well, my advice is *Beware the Manx Cat*.' And with that he flew off into the night with his 'Grrrrs' and 'Booos' and 'Arrghs' growing fainter and finally dying out altogether.

Manxmouse wondered what it was the Clutterbumph had meant, but he was growing tired and so he went on in the direction of the country smells until he came to the edge of Buntingdowndale where the pavement ended.

He walked on for a little while longer, enjoying the feel of grass and leaves and earth and twigs beneath his feet. Just as the moon was beginning to set and the stars to pale, Manxmouse found a soft spot under a hedge, curled up and went to sleep.

When he awoke it was broad daylight. The sun had been shining long enough to dry the dew from the grass and the flowers. It was warm and comfortable. As Manxmouse emerged from under his hedge, he saw that he was at a road junction with an old signpost leaning slightly askew. One fingerboard pointing to the right was marked LITTLE GREAT MUNDEN, and the other pointing to the left was lettered, NASTY. A Billibird perched on top of the signpost, manicuring its fingernails.

A Billibird carries a tail light, can fly backwards as well as forwards and sideways, and knows a great deal about a lot of things, but not everything.

The Billibird stopped doing its nails and said, 'Hello, a Manx Mouse! Or am I dreaming?'

It was strange, Manxmouse thought, how everyone he encountered seemed to know what he was, when he was not at all sure himself. He knew that he was a mouse, but not that kind of a one. For it must be remembered that as yet he had not seen himself.

'I was just wondering which way to go,' Manxmouse said.

'Well,' said the Billibird, 'you have a choice of one or the other. And you needn't worry, there's no Manx Cat either way. Little Great Munden has five houses in the

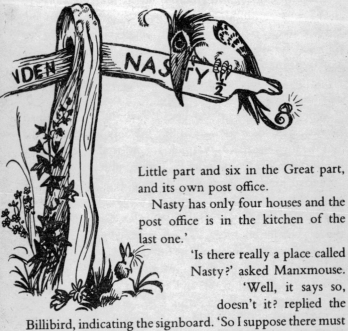

Little part and six in the Great part, and its own post office.

Nasty has only four houses and the post office is in the kitchen of the last one.'

'Is there really a place called Nasty?' asked Manxmouse.

'Well, it says so, doesn't it? replied the Billibird, indicating the signboard. 'So I suppose there must be. I know some villages with even funnier names. There's one called Pity Me and another Come-to-Good. And then there's the one you ought to know about. It's called Mousehole, although they pronounce it Mouzle. The villagers try to pronounce Nasty as Naystie, but it's Nasty all right, and there's nothing they can do about it.'

'It must be horrid, then,' Manxmouse suggested.

'Oh no, on the contrary, it's delightful—timbered houses with thatched roofs, early Elizabethan style, I take it; the most charming gardens and a pretty little pond. Nice people, too. I often go there myself."

'Then however did it get that name?' inquired Manxmouse.

'Now that is one of the things I don't know,' replied the Billibird, 'and there aren't many. Someone just called it that, and there it is.'

Manxmouse made up his mind. 'Then that, I think, is where I shall go for I'm getting hungry.'

'Mind,' said the Billibird, 'there'll be cats. But they're well fed and oughtn't to bother you, except maybe old One-Eye or Street Cat. But of course it's really Manx Cat you want to watch out for.'

The Billibird resumed its manicuring and as Manxmouse thanked it and went off down the road in the direction of Nasty, he heard it say, 'I'm not dreaming. I know I'm not. It actually is a Manx Mouse. Poor thing!'

Manxmouse wondered why, 'Poor thing'? For he was quite happy.

3

The Story of the Happenings in Nasty

Nasty was really exactly as the Billibird had described it: four charming cottages, the dark timbers showing bravely against the white plaster, and the eaves of the roofing thatches descending almost to the windows. The flowers in the gardens were just starting to bud.

The houses stood in a line on one side of the road and the pond the Billibird had mentioned was on the other, a blue patch of water with lily pads and rushes.

It was still early in the morning and no one was about. But the people of Nasty seemed to be the trusting kind, for two of the front doors were open and Manxmouse slipped into the first.

Following the good news told him by the odour in his nostrils, he had no difficulty in finding his way to the kitchen, or in climbing up the leg of the table where he found the remnants of a supper of bread and cheese, and a dish of rice pudding.

Manxmouse was sure nobody would mind, since he was so small that he would not be able to eat a great deal, just sufficient to satisfy his hunger. So he had some of each and it was all delicious.

He was sorry he had no pencil and paper to leave a

thank-you note, but he ate very tidily and cleared up the crumbs before he left. Then he slipped down the table leg and was just about to go by the way he had come, when he felt a sudden rush of air and then something soft and furry landed upon him. Two little paws with needle claws gripped him and the next thing he knew, he was held in the tiny but sharp teeth of a kitten and was being carried, still quite unharmed, into the neighbouring ironing room, where House Cat Mother with three more kittens was lying in a basket.

The kitten set Manxmouse down on the floor, put a paw on him and cried with enormous pride, 'Look, everyone! I've caught my first mouse, all alone, by myself! There I was in the kitchen, looking for my ping-pong ball that had rolled under the fridge when this mouse stepped out from behind the stove and threatened me. But I wasn't frightened, or intimidated, even though there was nobody there to help me. Keeping my head I gathered myself together, gave two waggles and avoiding the blow he aimed at me, made a tremendous spring, pounced and caught him. He put up a great fight, but I was too much

for him. And now I'm going to eat him all by myself.'

Manxmouse was too surprised to protest the exaggerations.

By this time House Cat Mother was up and out of her basket saying, 'You'll do nothing of the kind! What on earth have you got there?'

The kitten pressed its paw down harder on Manxmouse's back. 'My mouse!'

House Cat Mother came over and said, 'Why, it's blue! Can't you see it's poisonous! Get away from it, you stupid child!'

'But he's mine! I caught him and I want to eat him!'

At this House Cat Mother grew very angry and cuffed the kitten with her paw, knocking it head-over-heels. It

gave Manxmouse the opportunity to arise from his undignified position and catch his breath again, for he had been quite squashed.

'Eat him, you shan't!' the mother scolded. 'How many

34

times have I told you never to touch anything that isn't the right colour, taste or smell, or all three? Whoever heard of a blue mouse? Can't you see that this one would make you sick? Honestly, everything I say or try to teach you seems to go in one ear and out the other.'

'But I'm not poisonous!' Manxmouse protested, 'Really I'm not. Please, I promise you, you can eat me with the utmost safety. I didn't know I was blue, but if I am, I can't help my colour. It's quite harmless.'

House Cat Mother drew back from him and said indignantly, 'Well, I never heard of such a thing. A mouse actually asking to be eaten! That just proves he's bad and is trying to trap us. Come away at once, children!' and herding them together, she rushed them out of the room, leaving Manxmouse rather forlorn.

Was there really something the matter with him? And was it true that he was blue? And if so, what was wrong with that?

He remembered the pond across the road and thought that the thing to do was to go there and have a look at his reflection in it. He had hardly left the door of the cottage and proceeded to the side of the road, when once more there was a rush of air and a pounce, and he was caught up in a pair of powerful jaws.

And this time it wasn't a kitten but a ginger cat with but a single eye, the one Billibird had called Street Cat, or old One-Eye.

'Ha! Gotcha!' growled One-Eye. 'Thought I'd be sleeping, didn't you? They all fall for that one. Well, that's your tough luck. Goodbye, mouse! Some cats start eating at the head of the mouse, but I don't. I like to start with their tails as an appetizer and work on up, leaving the best part to the last.'

And with this he put one great paw on Manxmouse's head, when he suddenly leaped back with a cry of, 'What's this? Why, you haven't got a tail!'

'Haven't I?' said Manxmouse. 'I'm sorry, I didn't know.' Old One-Eye was upset. 'You're a Manx Mouse,' he said. 'Why didn't you say so? You should have told me immediately! Supposing I'd eaten you? You belong to

36

Manx Cat, and Manx Cat would have been furious with me if I'd eaten his mouse.'

Manxmouse said, 'But I don't understand! It's all so confusing! Who and what and where is Manx Cat? And where will I find him?'

Old One-Eye backed away still further, his fur standing up and his tail twitching. 'Phew!' he said, 'That was a narrow escape for me.' And then, 'Never you mind. You'll soon know the answer when you come across him. One thing I can tell you, you'll never get away from him. Manx Mice are meant to be eaten by Manx Cats. Enjoy yourself while you can.' And with that old One-Eye slouched off into the gardens behind the houses.

The pond across the street beckoned Manxmouse and he went over to see what he was really like.

It all seemed to be true. The breeze had died away and the surface of the pond was like a mirror, as Manxmouse crept down to the edge between two tall rushes and looked in. He was blue and indeed, had no tail. He turned this way and that to make sure of the latter— there was no mistake

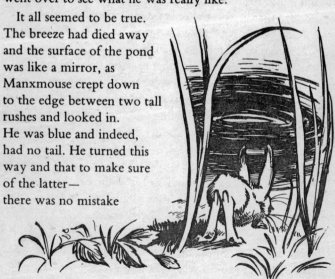

about the blue part—and even got himself afloat on a lily pad to be able to see better behind himself. He had just caught a glimpse of the little button where his tail should have been, when a deep voice rumbled, 'There's no use in your looking further, youngster, there isn't one,' and then it added, 'Burrp!'

Manxmouse looked around and saw a huge grey-green frog with popping eyes squatting on the bank watching him.

'That,' said Manxmouse, now prepared to make the best of things, 'is because I'm a Manx Mouse.' For it was clear to him at last that that was what and who he must be, since everyone had been calling him by this name. It had not come as too much of a shock to him. For he thought that the world must be full of Manx Mice like himself and had no idea that he was the only one in existence.

'Can you swim?' asked the frog and burped again.

'I'm not sure,' replied Manxmouse.

'Well then, you'd better get back off that lily pad. Manx Cat wouldn't like it if you were to drown. Burrp! Burrp!'

Manxmouse did as he was told because he didn't fancy drowning either, and then he said, 'Just who is this Manx Cat everyone is talking about? And where would I meet him?'

'Ho, ho!' rumbled the frog, 'That's a good one! The Manx Cat is a cat without a tail, and the first time you see him you'd better start running. Plain cats eat plain mice; Manx Cats eat Manx Mice. There you are, that's the rule.'

Manxmouse had now managed to creep back onto the shore and was sitting up wiping some droplets of water that had got onto his whiskers, and shaking his feet.

'You're certainly the queerest-looking specimen I ever saw,' commented the frog and added three burps for good measure. 'No tail, blue all over and as for those ears—Oh, burrp!'

Good-natured as Manxmouse was, he was becoming just a little fed up with comments on his shape and colour and so he said, 'I'm very sorry, but I can't help how I look. And, for that matter, don't you think you might appear a little odd yourself, with your eyes sticking out so that they're practically on top of your head?'

The frog now produced the largest of all his burps and said, 'Eyes on top of my head, eh? Well, I'll tell you something, youngster. It might be better for you if yours were, too, because you never know where trouble is coming from next.' And with that he dived plop into the pond and disappeared. It broke up the surface and sent ripples out in every direction. When they washed up onto the shore where Manxmouse was sitting, his image looked very funny and wavy indeed, like standing before one of those crazy mirrors at a fun fair. One moment he was fat and the next lean; his ears long and then short.

Then suddenly the reflection was darkened by a shadow, a great beating of wings, and a splash as something plummetted out of the sky and seized Manxmouse in talons of iron. The next moment he was flying dizzily through the air, with the earth spinning and tumbling about him. Feeling giddy he closed his eyes and did not open them again until there was a bump and he felt himself once more on ground.

He heard a voice say, "Now then, we'll just have a look at what we've got here.'

Gazing up, Manxmouse saw the head of an enormous bird with bright yellow eyes and a cruel, curved beak.

4

The Story of Manxmouse and Pilot Captain Hawk

PEERING down, the bird of prey inspected a creature such as he had never seen before in all his days of hunting from the sky. 'Hello,' he said, 'what on earth are you? No tail, funny feet, ears like a rabbit and blue all over. Are you mole, vole, mouse or shrew?'

Manxmouse, who was being terribly squashed, gasped, 'If you could just let me go a little, sir, I'd ...'

'Oh, sorry!' said the hawk, for such it was, 'Of course! I'd forgotten about my undercarriage. It's a bit powerful,' and he relinquished his grip.

Manxmouse sighed with relief and said, 'I'm a Manx Mouse and everyone says I'm going to be eaten by a Manx Cat. But for a moment I thought I was going to be eaten by you.'

'Well, I never! Why, it would be a shame to eat you. I'm probably the only hawk who's ever caught something like you. Nobody would ever believe me. There I was at three thousand feet, on a nice thermal—you know what a thermal is, don't you?'

'No, I don't,' Manxmouse admitted. For this was something his creator, the ceramist, would not have known either.

'Well, it's an up-current of air caused by heat rising. Catch a good one and you can float on it for hours. I was looking for a meal when I saw that frog. Clever fellow, he was too quick for me. I'd already started my dive—it's automatic, you know—and then I saw *you*.'

'You mean to say,' Manxmouse queried, amazed, 'that you can see a tiny thing like me from that high up?'

'Oh my goodness, yes,' exaggerated the bird, who, like most flyers was something of a show-off. 'Even higher: five thousand feet—ten thousand. We've got telescopic eyes. Well, on the way down I thought there was something odd about your colour, you know. It just sort of flashed through my mind. But I was doing about 500 mph —that's miles per hour—by that time and didn't want to bother to use my air brakes. It was as nice a strike as I've ever made, even though I did get my tail feathers wet on the pull out. So then when we were climbing again and I saw that you actually *were* blue, I thought to myself that we'd better have another little look-see. And so here we are, the two of us. Captain Hawk's the name, Senior Pilot.'

Manxmouse said politely, 'And I'm very pleased to meet you, Captain.'

'For that matter,' Captain Hawk replied, 'I'm very pleased to meet you as well. I shall be dining out on this for a long time—I don't mean dining out on YOU,' Hawk hastened to add, 'it's just a phrase and means having something to talk about when you're invited out to dinner. I shall certainly tell about having caught a Manx Mouse.

By the way, young fellow, have you ever flown before?'

'No, never—except for . . . just now . . .'

Captain Hawk laughed, 'Oh that! I wouldn't call that flying. How would you like a little flip? It's the least I can offer to make amends for having been just a trifle rough with you.'

'If it wouldn't be too much trouble,' said Manxmouse.

'No, no, not at all! Delighted, old sport! Always pleased to be able to take someone up on his first hop and get him air-minded. Now, climb up and pass along to the front of the aircraft—I mean, get up onto my head, where you'll find you'll be able to hang on and it's quite comfortable. Don't worry if you feel a trifle dizzy at first, you'll soon get used to it. And even if you were to fall off—not to worry. I'd catch you before you dropped very far.'

'Oh, I'm glad of that,' said Manxmouse.

And with this he boarded the bird at his tail and went along his back to a place just behind his head, where the feathers were rather thinner and he could get a firm grip with his fore paws.

Captain Hawk murmured, 'Fasten your seat belts, please and no smoking during take-off.'

'I beg your pardon,' said Manxmouse, 'what was that you said?'

Captain Hawk replied, 'Regulations. Hang on, now, we're off!' With that he gave a great leap upward with his strong legs and with a whoosh and a rush, his two powerful wings began to beat the air. As Manxmouse clung on tightly, the earth began to fall away beneath them, and he had to hold firmly because the ascent was so swift and slightly bumpy.

Hawk's head seemed to be on a swivel, for he turned it around to Manxmouse, looking over his shoulder and remarked, 'Take-off on full power. Twin engines, you know. It will be a lot steadier when I throttle back. If you get a funny feeling in your ears, swallow hard. I'm afraid we're out of sweets on this trip.'

It was all very confusing to Manxmouse, although anybody who has ever been on an airliner knows that the hostesses pass out boiled sweets to enable the passengers to swallow which takes the pressure of the sudden climb from their eardrums. Peering from either side of Hawk's neck he could secure the most wonderful view.

Not only was the earth continuing to drop away as though it were falling instead of them rising, but everything began to shrink. The buildings which had looked so enormous to Manxmouse were now like dolls' houses and dwindled until they were even smaller than Manxmouse himself. The roads were but thin lines and cars driving along them looked no bigger than beetles. The pond had diminished to the size of a single drop of water. But at the same time the boundaries of the earth had become enlarged and spread out like a coloured map, with

the fields cut into checker-board squares by stone walls and hedges.

Beneath them was the village of Buntingdowndale from where he had come. There was the tiny emerald patch of the village green, the church tower with its flag flying and the criss-cross of streets.

At the same time he could see the road junction like a 'V', where he had met the Billibird, though it was no longer possible to make out the signpost. There were four little dots which were now all that was left of the houses of Nasty.

Captain Hawk's wings were beating with less violence and the passage had become smoother. Whatever dizziness Manxmouse might have experienced at the beginning had passed. He had swallowed dutifully and his ears were no trouble, and he could now give himself up to the enjoyment of what was going on. What fun flying was!

'We've throttled back,' the Captain remarked. 'There are some cumulus clouds yonder. We'll go over and I'll show you a nice little trick.'

'What are cumulus clouds?' Manxmouse asked. Everything was so new and different. He had had some rather shattering experiences while on earth and up here in the sky it was wonderfully quiet and exciting, peaceful and thrilling all at the same time.

'Those big, white, thundery-looking ones,' Captain Hawk explained, and indicated a huge mountain of billowy white clouds rising straight up into the air, like packages of cotton wool piled one atop the other. 'There will be some nice up-draughts. The clouds cool at the top, you see, and the hot air rises from below. They're what we call "thermals". You watch—we'll cut our engines and . . .'

To Manxmouse's alarm the great wings on either side of him had stopped and he wondered whether something had gone wrong, or whether the Captain was ill. The stillness was frightening after the whir of their beating. But now, close to the edge of the towering, white clouds they suddenly shot up into the sky like an express lift in an office building.

'There,' said Hawk, 'isn't it fun? We can go as high as we like on one of these currents and then glide across to that cloud beyond, miles away, and pick up another. Tre-

mendous saving on fuel, and a nice, smooth ride.'

They rose on the column of warm air. Manxmouse thought what a wonderful thing it must be to be a hawk and be able to live up here in the quiet of the sky.

They went up higher and higher, until at last Captain Hawk wheeled in a wide circle. He said, 'I mustn't overdo it. I'm actually not licensed for passengers and so I don't carry oxygen equipment.'

'What's that?' Manxmouse queried.

'Oh, of course,' Captain Hawk explained, 'since you've never flown before you wouldn't know about that. The further up you go, the thinner the air. People who live on earth begin to feel very funny and have to have special tanks of oxygen and masks to breath properly. I don't, of course, because I'm used to it. My own ceiling is a good deal above this, but I don't want you to feel uncomfortable. Enjoying yourself?'

'Marvellously!' said Manxmouse. Beneath him the landscape of fields and woodlands with silver threads of streams and rivers, small towns and villages was un-reeling at dizzying speed as they flew down wind now.

Captain Hawk must have done a great deal of flying close to the big airliners criss-crossing the country, listening to what was being broadcast inside them, for he suddenly said, 'This is your Captain speaking. We are now cruising at an altitude of 7,000 feet; our air speed is 250 mph and we are overflying St Albans. Hello, there's a nice looking vole by that hedge. Pity I'm busy.'

'Can you *really* see tiny things down there on the ground?' Manxmouse asked again.

'Of course. I told you that's my speciality.' replied Hawk. 'There's a mother rabbit in that field below with six little ones, and a green grass snake just disappearing into some thorn. I see a mouse, but just an ordinary one, not an extraordinary chap like you. And there are three fat trout lazing in that brook we're just overflying.'

Manxmouse could not even make out the brook, much less any fish in it and marvelled, 'I can hardly see anything at all.'

'Oh, but I'll wager you've got good ears instead,' Hawk said and then added, 'Especially those long, rabbity ones. That's what you need to hear things coming—particularly things like Manx Cat.'

For the first time Manxmouse felt something like a cold shiver. He had been born without fear and so the Clutterbumph had had no power over him. But the constant repetition of the threat to his life by Manx Cat was beginning to have an effect. He had felt so happy, free, safe and secure up in the blue, but now he was reminded that somewhere below was Manx Cat.

'We're approaching central London,' Hawk said. 'That river you see winding in and out is the Thames, of course. We are now directly over Buckingham Palace, the Mall and Admiralty Arch. Westminster Abbey and the Houses of Parliament are on your right and that long thing sticking up is Nelson's column. We'll turn west now.'

Manxmouse forgot about Manx Cat once more in the fascination of the great grey city beneath, as Hawk banked steeply. He had started his engines again, or rather his wings, and they passed over roof tops, domes, spires and streets down which thousands of cars were crawling.

'People down there,' commented Captain Hawk, 'millions of them—some good, some bad. I avoid them all.'

'When you're always on the ground, as I am, I suppose you can't,' said Manxmouse.

The ceramist, of course, had known a great deal about people and so Manxmouse too knew what they were.

'Oh, they won't bother you if you keep out of their way,' said the Captain. 'But every so often if I come down too low, I encounter anti-aircraft fire. Hunters with shotguns.'

At last the grey houses began to thin out and suddenly they came upon a most curious place that seemed to be an enormous field of stone on which sat hundreds of silver birds, but not like Captain Hawk or Billibird, or any others he had seen.

'London Airport', his pilot commented.

'But what are all those birds down there?'

'Birds! Ha, ha, ha!' laughed the Captain. 'Those are aeroplanes, the things that people fly in. Here comes one now. We'll have a look at it.'

With a whoosh, a roar and a whine, an enormous four-engined jet passed by overhead to begin its descent, its vast expanse of wings blotting out the sun momentarily, and Manxmouse saw that its tail, instead of being flat like Hawk's, was as high as two houses one on top of another.

'Did you ever see anything so silly?' Captain Hawk said. 'They can't flap their wings; they can't soar or glide; they make a noise and they smell. And they call that flying!'

At that moment there was another strange noise: 'Rackety-rackety! Clattery-clattery!' Something that was a cross between a beetle, a dragonfly and a windmill whirled past them. Hawk had to veer off so sharply that Manxmouse was compelled to cling for dear life.

'What is it?' Manxmouse cried in alarm.

'Helicopter. Real crazy! I can't understand what holds it up. The other thing at least has wings, even though they're not *my* idea of wings. But that's only an egg-beater. I don't often come this way because it's too dangerous for a bird. I had a friend once who was sucked into one of those jet engines and that was the end of him. But I wanted you to have a look-see.'

He wheeled again, dropping one wing steeply so that the wind caught them as they turned and sailed them away so swiftly that in a moment the great airport below had vanished. 'We call this banking,' said Hawk. 'It's how you turn in the air. Well, I guess that's about enough for your first hop. Is there any place you'd like to go where I can drop you? Were you going somewhere when I—ah—picked you up?'

'Oh no,' said Manxmouse, 'I really don't mind. Anywhere will do.'

'Fine, then' said Hawk. 'We'll just get away from here, which is no place for a mouse anyway. I've a friend up near Pease Pottage I want to see and I'll let you off there. There's a film studio nearby incidentally, which you might like to visit.'

They turned northwards and as Hawk began to circle, the ground came up to meet them and everything that had been tiny suddenly began to grow larger and assume its normal shape and size—houses, trees, cars and even people in the fields.

'I should have liked to have shown you a power dive,' Hawk said, 'but you couldn't have stood the g's.'

'The g's?' said Manxmouse.

'Oh, I forgot, you're not a flyer,' Hawk said. 'My speed plus the force of gravity at the pull-out. The pressure on your insides makes you feel sick.''

'Well, I'm certainly glad you didn't,' said Manxmouse.

Hawk's voice changed again and he announced, 'This is your Captain speaking. In a few moments we will be landing at Croftsley Farm by Pease Pottage. Fasten your seat belts and no smoking, please. Passengers will kindly keep their seats until the aircraft comes to a stand-still. Please make sure that you have all your hand luggage. We hope you have enjoyed this flight.'

The field was now so close that Manxmouse could make out the blades of grass.

'Undercarriage down!' reported the Captain. There was a slight lift for an instant and then with hardly a jar they settled gently onto the ground.

Manxmouse dismounted as his pilot said, 'There you are. Hope you liked the ride.'

'Oh yes,' cried Manxmouse. 'It was absolutely wonderful. I do thank you. It was most good of you.'

'No, no, no,' said Captain Hawk, 'the pleasure was all on my side. Imagine my having given a blue mouse with no tail and rabbit ears his first flight! What a story I shall have to tell! Good luck, then and goodbye!' And with that he took off.

Manxmouse heard the beating of his wings and almost before he knew it, Captain Hawk was a tiny diminishing dot in the sky until he vanished altogether.

5
The Story of the Great Bumbleton
Mouse Hunt

Now Manxmouse was strolling along in the pleasant and well-tended, rolling farmland in which he had found himself deposited by Captain Hawk, reflecting upon his recent adventure and what a marvellous thing it was to fly. As he passed alongside the hedge that formed a boundary of a ploughed field, he heard a great hullabaloo in the distance. The wind carried to him the baying of hounds, and the rat-tat-tat of hooves. The sounds faded, grew louder and faded again and once Manxmouse, looking across the field to a wooded hill on the other side, saw red-and black-coated riders streaming by to vanish behind a copse, in the last hunt of the season.

Manxmouse went marching on, still thinking his own thoughts. Suddenly he became aware of the clatter and view-halloo growing louder and louder. It appeared to be approaching.

He sat up to listen, turning his too large, but at this point quite useful, rabbit ears in the direction of the sound. Sure enough the thunder of the horses' hooves was increasing and the winding of the horn, the yelping and baying of hounds, all were shattering the quiet of the peaceful countryside.

At this moment Manxmouse saw a flash of red and heard a crash in the undergrowth of the hedge just ahead of him, followed by heavy breathing. When he reached the spot he saw that it was a fox. It was lying on its side exhausted, its tongue lolling out of its mouth, its eyes miserable. As Manxmouse came up it was barely able to lift its head to have a look at him.

'That's right!' he gasped, 'Go ahead—Laugh at me. I don't blame you. I've had plenty of you chaps for breakfast, lunch and tea and now it's your turn. They'll be on me in a minute.'

The fox was one of the greatest enemies of mice, particularly their cousins in the field. Yet at this moment Manxmouse could only feel pity for this beautiful creature about to meet its end, as it lay there, its flanks heaving, its glassy eyes turned piteously upon him.

'But I don't want to laugh,' Manxmouse said.

The sounds of the hunt drew closer. 'I've had it,' said the fox. 'I've not been well lately, or I'd have run the legs off those clots. Imagine me, Joe Reynard, being caught by the Bumbleton Hunt—the worst pack in the county! I wouldn't care so much for my reputation, but it's for my family. I've got a lot of kids.'

And now three fields away and bursting from a clump of trees, Manxmouse could see the hounds running and riders beginning to appear in their wake.

'The Bumbleton hounds!' said the fox in disgust. 'Well, here's the end of me! You'd better get away from this spot, young fellow, for it's going to be a mess. They're such shockers I doubt if they'll even know how to finish me off properly.'

'Oh dear,' said Manxmouse, 'can't I help you in some way? Isn't there *anything* I could do?'

Joe Reynard was ready to grasp at any straw. He lifted his weary head. 'Could you take them off me for just a moment, while I catch my breath? I've got a hidey-hole about a half mile from here and if I could get to it . . .'

'Oh, I'd try,' Manxmouse said, 'but I wouldn't know how. What should I do?'

The baying and yelping sounded louder and louder.

'Here,' said Joe Reynard, 'take my handkerchief. It has

my scent on it. Beat off in any old direction and keep going. There isn't a brain cell working in the entire pack.'

He handed over the handkerchief. There was no more time for a further exchange. Manxmouse took it in his teeth, dived through the hedge and started running up the ploughed field in the direction from which all the hullabaloo was coming.

The hounds came streaming down another furrow, heading straight for the hedge, but when they reached there, General Hound, in command of the pack, held up his paw and shouted, 'Hold it, boys! Stop everyone! There's something wrong here!' The order was passed backwards from the Colonel Hound to Major Hound, to Captain Hound, to Lieutenant Hound, barked out loudly by Sergeant Hound, caught by Corporal Hound and finally reached the Privates.

'Hold it! Company halt! Some trouble up front.'

The General gave a sniff and said, 'There's a strong smell of fox right here, but then the scent suddenly goes off up there to the left. Do you make it that way, Colonel?'

General Hound was an old boy with a thousand wrinkles in his brow resulting from the state of confusion in which he usually found himself. Colonel Hound's problem was that he was prone to hay-fever that interfered with his sniffing and so he usually just agreed with what the General said. Major Hound was all spit and polish and so interested in his own appearance and keeping himself looking smart that he rarely if ever knew in which direction the fox had gone. The Captain and the Lieutenant didn't like hunting

and wanted to be house pets. The only one who was of any use was Sergeant Hound and his legs were beginning to give out.

All the hounds had now collected around the General who said, 'If it's old Joe Reynard, it would be just like him to pull some kind of trick.'

'Oh, it's Joe all right,' said the Colonel, 'By dose bay be blocked up, but I caught a glips of hib back there in

the woods. I'd dough hib anywhere.'

'Well, he won't get way from us this time,' said the General. 'Now, as to which way he went, what's your opinion, Major?'

The Major was busy worrying a burr out of one of his long, lop ears. 'Eh? What, what?' he said. 'Yessir! I agree with you absolutely one hundred per cent!'

The Captain whispered to the Lieutenant, 'Aw, I wish they'd call it off and let us go home.'

Sergeant Hound was barking orders to the Privates: 'All right, you chaps! Spread out a bit and see what you can pick up.'

At this point Squire Ffuffer drew up with his Chief Huntsman Sprigg and the rest of the ladies and gentlemen on their horses.

The Squire was aptly named, for he was too fat to be sitting on a horse, if you were to ask the horse on which he was sitting. He fuffed when he got excited. He was excited now. 'Fuff, fuff, fuff, what's got into those beasts? What are they all milling about like that for? What's up, Sprigg?'

The Huntsman who was as thin and pale with a long, lean jaw as Squire Ffuffer was fat and red said, 'I don't know, sir. They seem to be confused.'

'Well then—fuff, fuff—deconfuse them. Do something!'

Sprigg called out, 'Come on, General! Seek! Seek! Get in there, Colonel! Find, Major!'

The hounds paid no attention whatsoever.

'In my opinion,' the General was saying, 'he's gone and doubled back on us, up thataway.'

A very young Private who, as a matter of fact, had just been allowed to join the pack a week before, said, 'I think he's in there, under that hedge, sir.'

The General turned upon him furiously, 'Quiet!' he shouted, 'I'm the one here who's paid to think. I say he's gone away up to the left. All those in favour say "Aye"'.

There was a chorus of 'Ayes' led by the Colonel.

The General shouted, 'Okay, then boys! This way! Follow me!' and up he went, along the furrow behind Joe Reynard's handkerchief Manxmouse was carrying, a good hundred yards up ahead of them now.

The Huntsman shouted a few words of encouragement, sounded his horn and turning his steed, galloped after the hounds who were now baying happily once more as the scent of the handkerchief reached them. Behind came Squire Ffuffer bouncing up and down upon his horse and the rest of the Field.

Although Manxmouse had never taken part in a fox hunt, or what had now turned into a mouse hunt, before, of one thing he was certain. He had neither the length, the legs, the wind nor the stamina to outrun a pack of hounds, no matter how inept they might be. However, his only purpose was to gain a little time to allow Joe Reynard to recover sufficiently to reach his hidey-hole. And so, having got to the end of the furrow, he leaped over several ridges and ran down another in the direction from which he had come, passing the hunt in full cry on the way up.

Again at the edge of the field there had to be a halt and a consultation, until General Hound came to a decision. By that time Manxmouse was already going up yet another parallel furrow the other way.

And now the amazed farmers, spectators, followers and travellers in cars who had halted by the roadside to watch, were treated to the astonishing spectacle of the Bumbleton Hunt riding up and down from one end of a ploughed field to the other.

However, as indeed was inevitable even though he had had a head start of a hundred yards or so, the pack began to gain on Manxmouse and soon they were all in the same line. Besides which Manxmouse was getting out of breath and so when he reached the end of the field by the hedge, he simply stopped running and sat down to await their arrival.

The breeze carried the strong scent of the handkerchief to the General who shouted, 'Hurrah! Come on, boys! Follow me! We've got him now!'

'Hurrah! Hurrah!' shouted his army behind him and went charging down the field only to be compelled to skid to a stop in a cloud of dirt as the General applied all four brakes and came to a grinding halt on his haunches.

'Well, I'll be blowed!' For with his brow contracted in several dozen more wrinkles than ever before, he found

himself looking down upon such a creature as he had never before encountered. 'Colonel, gentlemen and others, gather around. See what we've caught this time.'

All the hounds did so and soon were sitting about in a circle with Manxmouse in the centre. He had very cleverly hidden Joe Reynard's handkerchief under a clod.

'I say,' said General Hound, 'won't the Hunt be proud when they see what we've turned up? Just look at it—it'll make the Bumbleton pack famous all over the world.'

'Extraordinary!' snuffled the Colonel.

'Sensational! said the Major, giving his whiskers a brush.

'Maybe now they'll let us go home,' chorused the Captain and the Lieutenant.

The Sergeant said, 'Attention, everyone! Three cheers for the General!'

The very young Private remarked, 'What is it? A mole?'

'What's that?' roared the General, 'A mole . . . Ridiculous! The colour's all wrong to begin with—it's blue. Notice the hind legs. And those ears . . . I suppose the Huntsman will accuse us of having gone after a rabbit. But I do still get a very strong fox scent.'

He leaned over and put his nose down quite close and asked, 'Just what are you supposed to be?'

'I'm a Manx Mouse.'

The General recoiled at the mouse part of the word and decided to ignore it. 'Boys!' he called out, 'You're to be congratulated. We've caught a Manx!'

The Sergeant again called, 'Three cheers for the General!'

Now the ladies and gentlemen of the Hunt, led by Squire Ffuffer and Huntsman Sprigg had still four ploughed furrows to go before they would catch up. But they heard the cheering and saw the hounds collected in a circle and Squire Ffuffer cried, 'They've got him! We shall be in at the kill! Faster, everyone!'

The General continued to interrogate Manxmouse: where he came from; what kind of an animal he was; why his hindlegs looked like those of a kangaroo and his body like that of an opossum; and in particular, why there was such a strong scent of fox about him.

'Oh, as to that,' Manxmouse said, 'that's Joe Reynard's handkerchief. He gave it to me to put you off. It wasn't fair because he wasn't feeling well. By now he'll be safe in his hidey-hole.'

'He isn't,' said the youngest Private. 'He's right over there, under the hedge. I heard someone laughing.'

'Shut up!' ordered the Sergeant, 'Can't you see the General's talking?'

'His handkerchief!' the General said, 'I say, that was jolly clever of him, and jolly clever of you, too. We haven't had such a splendid chase as this in years. I don't mind his getting off, particularly when I think how pleased the Squire will be when he sees you. Attention now, boys! Here they come.'

Everybody shouted, 'Attention!' from the Colonel down to the Sergeant, with the exception of the Privates who had no one to shout to.

And indeed the horses were now coming galloping down from the bottom of the field with Squire Ffuffer in high fettle crying, 'Yoiks! In at the kill! And you shall have his brush, Miss Blenkinsop.'

For it seems that the Squire, who was a widower, was rather sweet on Miss Blenkinsop, one of the young ladies of the Hunt.

'Oh!' said she, 'Do you really mean it? It will be my first one.'

'And well deserved, my dear,' replied the Squire, and with his elbows joggling and his seat bouncing up and down on his poor horse, he gave full rein to where his pack at last had run something to ground.

As he approached, Sergeant Hound gave a command 'Attention! Divide! Hup . . . One . . . two!'

The pack of Privates neatly split in two to make a line opening up to where General Hound proudly stood alongside Manxmouse. As the Squire rode up he saluted smartly and said, 'Ah there, Squire, welcome! And may I be the first to congratulate you on this very special day! We've caught you a Manx.'

The Squire reined in so sharply that Miss Blenkinsop almost ran into him. 'You've caught me a what?' he cried.

'A Manx, sir.'

At this Miss Blenkinsop, who had had a good look, screamed, 'Why, it's nothing but a mouse! And a horrid one, too!'

'Fuff, fuff, fuff,' the Squire fuffed, 'Do you mean to say that I and the Bumbleton Hunt have been riding up and down these blinking furrows all morning chasing a mouse?'

'But he's a most extraordinary one,' said the General, 'Isn't he, Colonel?'

'Bost extraordinary,' agreed the Colonel, whose nose was now entirely blocked up.

'Why, look at him! Did you ever see a mouse with ears like a rabbit, feet like a kangaroo, and blue all over? Besides which, he's done the most extraordinary things. He's had a flight over London with Captain Hawk; met a

66

Clutterbumph and seems to belong to someone or something called Manx Cat. Most amazing story, what, Colonel?'

'Bost.'

Miss Blenkinsop suddenly burst into tears. 'Oh dear,' she cried, 'and you promised me my first brush!'

In an absolute fury Squire Ffuffer fuffed, 'And by Jiminy, you shall have it! Huntsman Sprigg, cut off the tail of whatever it is.'

Miss Blenkinsop screamed again and then said, 'I don't want his nasty old tail!'

'Fuff, fuff! Cut it off, I say! We'll have something to show for this day.'

Huntsman Sprigg dismounted, drew his knife and marched over to Manxmouse. 'Turn around,' he said.

Manxmouse did so.

'Sir,' Sprigg reported, 'I'm afraid it hasn't got a tail.'

'There you are!' said the General, 'Aren't you pleased? He's a genuine Manx.'

The young Private said, 'There's Joe now. I can see him, under the hedge. He's rolling on the ground, holding his sides. Look!'

'Pipe down!' barked the Sergeant. 'Who wants an old fox when we've captured something like this for the Squire? We'll all get double rations tonight.'

But the Squire was not all that pleased. In fact he was furious and it took him three minutes of pure fuffing before he could get the words out. 'You idiots! You imbeciles! You dimwits! Can't you see that you've made fools of me and the Bumbleton Hunt? We shall never live this down! I order this hunt called off.' He jumped the hedge and galloped off.

As Sprigg sounded the long note of 'Going Home', General Hound shrugged and said, 'There's just no pleasing some people. Personally I'm pretty proud of myself and you boys, and you're all promoted in memory of this day —me to Field Marshal.' To Manxmouse he said, 'Well, goodbye, old chap and happy to have made your acquaintance. You've given us some dashed fine sport and behaved most admirably. If you see Joe Reynard, give him our respects and say we hope he'll be feeling better shortly. All right, Sergeant, give the orders.'

The Sergeant barked, 'Attention! Close ranks! About

face! At the jog, march!' And following Mr Sprigg the Huntsman, the from now on famous, mouse-hunting Bumbleton pack loped off.

Nor did Manxmouse have any difficulty in locating Joe Reynard, for the fox was still lying on his back under the hedge with his arms wrapped about himself, so that in alarm he ran over and said, 'Oh, Mr Reynard, are you all right? Have you a cramp?'

'Cramp!' shrieked the fox, 'My sides ache! I've never laughed so much in my life. The Bumbleton pack and the whole caboosh trailing up and down that ploughed field! I thought I'd die! Pal, you were brilliant, marvellous, fab! Put it there!' Sitting up, grinning from ear to ear, he extended his paw which Manxmouse shook solemnly.

'You're sure you're not feeling too ill?' Manxmouse said anxiously. 'You know, you said you weren't well.'

'Never felt better in my life!' said the fox. 'There's no cure like laughter. I'd ask you up to the house to meet the missus and the kids, but we're just redecorating at the moment and everything's full of paint. But I'll never forget you, chum. The next field mouse I catch, I'll let go, dedicated to you. Thanks again.' And with this he went trotting off under the hedge until he came to the edge of the woods, into which he disappeared with a final farewell flirt of his red brush.

The most interesting things do seem to happen to me, thought Manxmouse and continued on his way.

6

The Story of Nervous Nelly

AFTER walking some distance, Manxmouse sat down to
rest again by the side of the road. Ahead of him lay the
brow of a hill. The country now was rather more like
a park with huge spreading trees and large estates, with
somewhat grand houses.

At that moment two fellows on bicycles approached
one another. They were workmen dressed in rough clothes
and one appeared over the skyline of the hill coasting
down, while the other was climbing. When they met right
opposite where Manxmouse was sitting by the trunk of a
beech tree, they stopped. The one going uphill said to
the one descending, ''Ullo mate, what's up?'

The other replied, 'No use your going on, we're laid off.'

'What's wrong now?'

'Nelly.'

'What, again?'

'Yep.'

'What's got into 'er this time?'

'Nerves. When they went to fetch 'er for the scene, she
was lying down and wouldn't get up.'

'Bloomin' nuisance, that's what I call 'er. 'Ad to call off

shootin' for the day.'

'Coo, you wouldn't see me take on a primmy-donny like that. Wastin' a lot of money and me time, too.'

The downhill man said, 'What d'you care? We get pyde whether she works or not.'

'It's the principle of the thing. 'Oldin' everything and everybody up because she's a bloomin' hysteric. Where were they at now?'

'The picnic scene where she's supposed to come barging in and bust it up. Stage 4. She wouldn't budge. The Producer's 'aving a fit; the Director's tearing 'is 'air and it's the rest of the day off with pay for everybody on the set.'

Uphill said, 'If it was me, I'd take a stick to 'er.'

Downhill laughed, 'That you wouldn't! You ain't seen Nelly when she gets it into 'er 'ead to be narky. What about a pint and a game of darts at The Sword and Feather?'

'Right you are, mate!' Uphill turned his bicycle around and the two men rode off together, leaving Manxmouse to wonder what it was all about.

Who was Nelly? Why was she nervous? Whose time and money were being wasted? What could it all mean? And then he remembered that Captain Hawk had said there was a film studio near by. And now something else that the downhill cyclist had mentioned came into Manxmouse's head, namely that they had been about to film a scene of a picnic in which this Nelly was to appear. So Nelly, then, must be a movie star. At picnics there were usually good things to eat; there might still be some food about and Manxmouse was hungry again. There is nothing like flying and excitement to stir up one's appetite. And anyway, what lay ahead seemed much more interesting than the other direction.

So Manxmouse went over the hill and into the broad valley on the other side, where he came to a large collection of buildings and a gate over which was the name: 'FLICKER STUDIOS. No Admittance.'

There was a gatekeeper stopping cars going in, inquiring into people's business and asking them to show passes and what-not. But this was no problem to Manxmouse who simply ran around behind a fancy Rolls Royce which was receiving a particularly ceremonious salute, nipped through the gates and on down a street lined on both sides with cavernous buildings.

It was really a most interesting place and Manxmouse would have stopped longer to see, for there were actors and actresses walking about, made up and wearing all sorts of costumes. Some were dressed up as pirates, others as gentlemen in powdered wigs, knee-breeches and long-tailed coats. There were cowboys, generals, Africans, sailors, anything and everything one could imagine. But Manxmouse was more interested in finding Stage 4.

This was actually not too difficult. All Manxmouse had to do was to keep out from underfoot of actors, property men, clapperboard boys, script girls, producers, directors and proceed along the sides of buildings marked 1, 2 and 3 until he came to number 4.

He went inside. There he had to climb over a great tangle of cables, ropes and wires laid out on the floor. Standing by a camera, a tall man in spectacles was having a row with a short, fat man with a brownish skin who had something like a towel wrapped around his head. And, of course, the subject was Nelly.

The tall man said, 'If you don't have her on the set here at nine o'clock tomorrow morning, you're both sacked!'

Manxmouse felt very sorry for Nelly. But by this time he had had a whiff of something rather good, and following the cables, he came upon the picnic set which fortunately had not been dismantled.

It was astonishing how lifelike it was, how much it resembled the real country. There was a knoll and a spreading oak tree and bushes and flowers and rocks. Only everything was artificial and made of plaster or lath, cloth, rubber or papier-maché, except for the picnic spread out on a white cloth beneath the oak. This was absolutely real. With no one paying any attention, since the set was wholly deserted, Manxmouse had a good tuck in.

He had some hard-boiled egg, a bit of brown bread and butter, a portion of excellent Wensleydale cheese and there were some tasty sweet biscuits and delicious chocolate layer cake.

Whatever the reason for the attack of nerves on Nelly, Manxmouse was most grateful, and having eaten all that he could hold, he went off searching for a spot where could rest.

By now all the lights had been put out and it was dark inside the building. He had to feel his way along until he came to a place where there was straw a foot deep on the floor, perfect for hiding and snoozing. Into this he crawled and contentedly went to sleep.

When he awoke next morning Manxmouse, peering up through the straw, was aware that there was something quite odd going on. In the first place he could see a most enormous grey shape with legs like the pillars that hold up buildings. Then he saw a nose that started like a nose but grew longer and longer and narrower and narrower, until at the end it looked like a piece of garden hose.

Equally strange was the fact that sitting cross-legged in the straw in the corner of the enclosure was the fat brown man whom Manxmouse had seen before. In his lap he was holding and plucking a *sitar*, which is an Indian musical instrument not unlike an electric guitar in shape, and he was singing to the enormous beast: 'Pearl of my heart, jewel of my soul, thou art more beautiful than the dawn, more clever than the great God Siva', and then stopping his plucking, he asked plaintively, 'Why won't you work?'

'Because I don't want to,' replied the beast, talking through the end of its nose which it used rather like a speaking trumpet. 'They ask me to do such silly things. Besides which, I'm nervous and frightened with all those lights and people shouting and those glass eyes staring at me.'

The brown man plunked his *sitar* again and sang,

'Moon of my existence, Sun of my life, Queen of the night, Empress of the day, harken to one who loves you.' And once more he coaxed, 'Won't you please work? There's nothing to be afraid of and besides, if you don't we'll be discharged and then neither of us will be able to eat.'

'That's your look-out,' replied the beast, 'I didn't ask to come here. I told you all those people frighten me and I'm going to stay frightened. And I wish you'd go and play that thing somewhere else, for it's beginning to give me a headache.'

The fat brown man did one more plunk, singing, 'Scent of lotus flower, spices of sandalwood, breath of my nostrils, you are bringing great sadness to my stomach.' But he rose and tucking his instrument under his arm, said, 'Very well then, I shall go and leave you to reflect upon the unhappiness you are inflicting upon me.' With that he left the enclosure and as he went, Manxmouse heard the beast mutter something that sounded like, 'Good riddance! Now perhaps we can have a little peace around here.'

At that moment Manxmouse, no longer able to contain his curiosity, popped right up out of the straw.

The beast who towered above him looked down at him out of one eye that gleamed behind long, curling lashes and said, 'Hello! Who are you?'

'I'm Manxmouse.'

'You're what?'

'Manxmouse, sir.'

'Not sir, if you don't mind. Madam!' And then she added, 'You mean you're a real mouse?'

'Oh yes indeed, I promise you I am,' Manxmouse

replied and then quickly added, 'Madam', not only for politeness, but for safety's sake for he had never seen such an enormous what-ever-it-was.

'There's something very wrong here.'

'Oh,' said Manxmouse, 'I hope I haven't done anything . . .'

'Not yet, you haven't. But you say you're a mouse?' the beast said, 'Come a bit closer, so I can have a better look at you. I simply can't believe it.'

Manxmouse did as he was asked, sitting on top of the straw to come under the glare of the eye looking down upon him. 'I know,' he said, to get it in before he should have to hear it again, 'wrong colour—I'm blue and I haven't a tail. I'm a funny shape; my feet aren't quite right and my ears are certainly all wrong. But nevertheless, I am a mouse.'

'Well, you may knock me over with a palm leaf!' said the animal. 'Do you know the story about us?'

'No, I'm afraid I don't. Which one?'

'About us being terrified of mice? Well, it's true. Or at least I am, and always have been. Now I'm going to ask you a question.'

'Yes, Madam, please do,' said Manxmouse.

'Why am I not afraid of you?'

Manxmouse replied, 'I'm sure I don't know, except that no one ought to be afraid of me. I wouldn't hurt anyone. I couldn't.'

'It isn't to be believed,' said the animal. 'There you are down there and here I am up here, and I'm not even shivering, not the teeniest sign of a quake. See here, you you wouldn't run up into my trunk, would you—ever?'

76

So that long nose was called a trunk. Manxmouse could think of nothing he cared to do less than run up it, for now he saw that there were two small holes at the end of it. If it was anything like a garden hose, it was a double one. 'Oh no, never!'

'Or crawl over my feet and tickle them?'

Then those tremendous pillars were actually legs and surely one wouldn't want to tickle a foot and be stamped upon and squashed flat. 'Certainly not!'

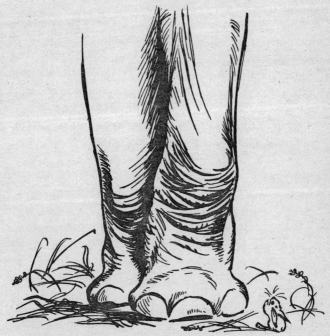

'Or make rustles in the straw? I can't bear little noises!'

'I'd try not to. I'd be as quiet as a . . .'

77

'Mouse!' concluded the thing. 'There! I've said the word looking at you, and I'm still not shivering, shaking, quaking or trembling. Something marvellous is happening to me! I hereby invite you to stay with me for ever to prove to one and all that I'm the only Nellyphant in captivity who isn't afraid of a mouse. Come a little closer and let me touch you with the tip of my trunk. Ha! Not so much as a shudder. That's the bravest thing I ever did in my life. There, it's true! You see? I'm simply not the least bit scared.'

'What did you say you were?' Manxmouse inquired. The touch of the tip of the animal's trunk had been cool, gentle and soft and not at all unpleasant.

'A Nellyphant,' she replied. 'At least that's what they call me. Nelly for short. You may call me Nelly and I shall call you Manxmouse, or perhaps just Mouse.'

'Oh, I'd like that very much indeed,' said Manxmouse. 'For it would make me feel—well—more like I ought to be.'

Nelly said, 'How would you like to get up onto my back?'

'You mean climb up your leg?' Manxmouse asked.

Nelly suddenly shifted one of her feet nervously. Brave she was, but this was the most astonishing and never-before-encountered situation and she still was not absolutely certain that she was prepared to let a real mouse climb up her leg, at least not yet. 'Well, not exactly,' she said, 'but hold still and I'll put you there.'

Nelly picked him up with the utmost delicacy with the tip of her trunk. She curled it around his body, and set him upon her back, or rather just behind her head in between

her two large ears, which to Manxmouse seemed about the size of tablecloths.

Nelly gave a tremendous gurgle of delight and began to shuffle both her forefeet in a kind of dance of celebration, lifting one after the other and singing, 'Oh joy! Oh happiness! I have a mouse sitting on my back and I'm not afraid. I'm the bravest Nellyphant in the world! Oh rapture! Oh gladness! I wish they could see me back in India now. Oh bliss! Oh ecstacy!'

79

Manxmouse too, felt pleased and thrilled because he was the sort of mouse who liked to be loved and who enjoyed giving happiness. It was rather exciting as well to find

oneself on a Nellyphant's back and while the view was not as broad as when he had been up with Hawk, still he could see a great deal more than from beneath the straw.

He saw that they were down at one end of Stage 4, where a kind of pen had been built. There Nellyphant was chained to a stake by one hind leg. The chain was jingling

merrily as she danced and sang.

The little fat, brown man suddenly appeared from around a corner without his *sitar* and saw to his surprise the change that had come over Nelly. He cried to her, 'Star of the universe! Light of the ages! Have you reflected?'

'Yes, yes,' Nelly replied, 'I shall work, for I am no longer afraid. I'm the bravest Nellyphant that ever was.'

The brown man, too, gave a cry of delight and began to dance and clap his hands. 'My beauty! My love! My wise one! My gift of heaven! You have made me the happiest of men and the most fortunate to be the possessor of such a gem set in the purest of gold.' And then loosening the chain around the Nellyphant's hind foot, he clapped his hands and shouted, 'Ho, everyone! Return! All is well! We shall work. Nelly has just informed me that she is nervous no longer and will carry out your commands.'

At this there was a great rush and trampling of feet throughout the echoing confines of Stage 4 as they all came running back to take their places on the set: the electricians, the plumbers, the carpenters, the property men, script girls, directors, producers, actors, actresses, clapper boys, light men, sound and camera men. Nelly was led forth by her owner, still gurgling joyously.

Manxmouse said, 'But what shall I do? Where shall I go?'

Nelly curled her trunk back over her head so that she could telephone to Manxmouse, 'Stay where you are. If you get down just behind my left ear, nobody will ever see you. But I'll know you're there, my new-found friend and mouse.'

*   *   *   *   *

And thereafter everything went absolutely swimmingly with the scene. The actors and actresses took their places.

No one noticed that there was one hard-boiled egg, a slice of brown bread and butter, a wedge of Wensleydale cheese, a biscuit and a piece of chocolate cake missing from the picnic. The Director took up his position. Camera men hunched and gazed through their eyepieces.

The Director said, 'Now, you all know what you're to do. Tom, you're handing Angela a lettuce and tomato sandwich when the elephant barges in. Let's run through it once.'

They did so and it was so perfect that the Director said, 'That's fine. We'll shoot it.'

The big arc lights sputtered, hissed and blazed. A boy stepped in front of the camera with a clapperboard slate on which was written:

```
SCENE 57
TAKE ONE
```

Then he gave the top of the board, which was hinged, a smart slap and retired, after which the Director shouted, 'Quiet, please, everyone!' and then, 'Roll 'em!'

The actors and actresses made believe to be enjoying their picnic. At a signal Nelly came charging into the scene, being careful not to step on anyone, and the picnickers scattered, with the exception of Tom and Angela who were pretending to be so in love that they didn't notice an elephant. This was supposed to be a kind of a joke.

'Cut!' cried the Director and then said, 'That was fine.'

Nelly whispered to Manxmouse, 'Isn't this fun?' and 'How did I look? How did I do?'

Manxmouse whispered back, and it was no problem since he was right behind Nelly's ear, 'I think you were wonderful! I'm sure I would be frightened to do that in front of all those people.'

'Well, I'm not,' said Nelly, 'and won't ever be again. At least not as long as you're with me to remind me how brave I am.'

After that they did another take just for luck, and then got down to the business of close-ups and different angles, which took up a lot of time and patience but Nelly didn't mind at all. When the day's work was over, the Director patted Nelly, praised her and gave her a large bun, a part of which she managed to slip to Manxmouse without anyone seeing or suspecting. To the brown man the Director said, 'What's got into her? She was sensational today—absolutely sensational!'

'I played my *sitar* to her and sang sweetly. She loves me and will do anything I ask.'

This caused Nelly fairly to shake with laughter.

The Director said, 'You must have hit a couple of sour notes yesterday and the day before. But never mind, if she keeps on like this, we'll catch up and might even go ahead of schedule.'

And so it would seem it was about to happen, for no elephant ever behaved better in a film the next three days, or obeyed commands with more patience. Nobody ever guessed that there was a Manx Mouse hidden behind her left ear, whispering to her and reminding her that she was the one Nellyphant in the world that wasn't frightened of a mouse and hence not afraid of anything else either.

At night, when her owner, who was an Indian by the name of Abdul Rahim Lal Popadur Mohammed Ali Khayyam but who was called Lalipop for short, went home leaving Nelly chained up, fed and watered, she would tenderly lift Manxmouse down from behind her ear and share her supper with him. In addition to her hay and because everyone was so pleased with her, she received all kinds of titbits which included apples, carrots, popcorn, lumps of molasses and brown sugar.

It was strange that for all their tremendous difference in size, they should both like the same kind of food and sweets, but there it was. It would have done one's heart good to have been there in the dark, listening to the suckings and chewings and gurglings and gnawings and yummings with occasional whispers of, 'Have a bit more of this, it's delicious', and, 'No thank you, I don't believe I could, I'm simply full up. But do try this candied peanut cluster, it's absolutely super.'

Finally, stuffed and drowsy, their chat about the events of the day died away and they went to sleep; Nelly standing up, Manxmouse curled between her forefeet.

All this might have gone on indefinitely, or at least until the film was finished, had not Abdul Rahim Lal Popadur Mohammed Ali Khayyam had a dream that he had not fastened Nelly securely. Waking up he could not remember whether it had been a dream, or true. So, picking up a torch he came to have a look. As he shone the light it fell full upon Manxmouse, fast asleep between two of Nelly's enormous feet. She too, had her eyes closed and was swaying to and fro, as Nellyphants do when they sleep standing up.

'Allah, preserve us!' cried Lalipop, seized a broom, raised it and brought it down upon Manxmouse with a tremendous swat.

Or rather, it came down upon the place where Manxmouse had been, for when the broom hit, he was not there. Mice are so sensitive to sound or to a disturbance, even in their sleep, that as the broom descended, Manxmouse slipped around behind Nelly's left leg.

In the first momentary shock of the discovery, Lalipop had no time to notice the colour was blue, the tail missing, the ears all wrong and the expression sweet. He only knew that it was a mouse and that if Nelly saw it there was no telling what would happen in her panic. She might break her chain and go charging through the studio, wrecking everything in her path and bringing disaster upon all of them.

In his excitement, Lalipop shouted, 'Ho! Ha!' as he beat at the straw with his broom, until Nelly woke up and opened her eyes to see what was going on. It did not take her long to become aware of the situation. The squeaks coming from her friend as he rushed about in the straw trying to avoid the blows raining down, left no doubt.

'What are you doing, you fool? Stop it!' Nelly cried, and aimed a whack at Lalipop's head with her trunk.

'Light of my life, have no fear!' cried the Indian, ducking, since he was used to doing so when Nelly became irritated with him. 'I'm here,' and he continued to rain thunderous blows upon the straw all about, as Nelly began to shout:

'Stop it! That's my mascot, my Manx Mouse! I'm not

86

afraid of him! We're friends!'

But in his excitement, Lalipop only heard the words 'mouse' and 'afraid' and in his turn shouted, 'Be calm, my Divinity! I shall protect you! In a moment I will have him.'

'Thump! Whack! Whoomph!' went the broom in every direction. Faster and faster came the blows, in addition to which the man was trampling the straw with his feet and Manxmouse was forced to flee for his life, or he surely would have been crushed. There was no time even to squeak, 'Goodbye' to Nelly. Gaining the side of the enclosure, he ran along to the door, dashed through and away down the floor of the stage, leaping over the wires and cables.

In his ears was still the sound of the blows of the broom and then a despairing trumpet from Nelly, 'You've driven away my Manx Mouse! Stupid idiot! You've had the last day of work you'll ever get out of me! I was the only Nellyphant who wasn't afraid of a mouse and now I'm all nervous and shaky again.'

Manxmouse reached the end of the stage, found the door open and was out into the night, down the street, through the gates, around the corner and off. The very last thing he heard was a final trumpet from Nelly, 'He was my friend! And now the Manx Cat will get him.'

Manxmouse ran as fast and far as he could, until he no longer could stir a limb. He had regained the country and crawled into the cranny of a stone wall.

There he remembered what he had heard Nelly say— 'And now the Manx Cat will get him.' He shivered inside the little niche of rock and hoped that the morning would come soon.

7

The Story of Wendy H. Troy

AND exactly eight hours later, for all this had taken place shortly after midnight, Manxmouse found himself in the pocket of a girl named Wendy H. Troy, on his way to school with her.

The 'H' in the name actually did not belong to her, since she had no middle name. But she was a lonely child with not many friends and so she had invented someone called Harrison, and put him between her first and second names. She only used the 'H' part on pieces of paper she could destroy, or when nobody could see.

The reason she was lonely was that she preferred the things she pretended to those that were real. This made her quiet but also very busy. People did not understand her and the other children thought that she was strange.

And how it came about that Manxmouse found his way into her pocket was the following:

Wendy H. Troy was walking along the lane with her books under her arm on the way to school, when she happened to see Manxmouse sitting on a twig by the side of the road, thinking.

And how this had come to be was equally simple. After escaping from the man with the broom, Manxmouse had fallen asleep inside the stone wall, to be awakened by the sun. When he crawled out, he discovered that he must have run a long way the night before. There was no sign of the film studio or Nelly, or Lalipop, or anyone at all. And since he did not know where he was he thought the best thing to do was to come out from his little cave into the warmth, sit down and think.

He had just begun when he heard footsteps and looking up, saw a face bending over him. In the face was a pair of bright hazel-green eyes with long lashes. Straight brown hair fell on either side of it. It belonged, he saw, to a small girl who cried, 'Oh! How pretty you are.'

'Do you *really* think so?' Manxmouse was overwhelmed. It was the first time that anyone had ever said that to him.

'Oh yes,' said the girl, 'I think you're beautiful. May I pick you up?'

'Yes, please do,' said Manxmouse. Thereupon he was lifted tenderly and cuddled in the palm of a soft hand, while with one finger she gently stroked his head and then held him to her cheek for a moment murmuring, 'Oh, I think you're just too sweet. What are you?'

'I'm a Manx Mouse.'

'How do you do, Manxmouse,' the girl said gravely. 'My name is Wendy H. Troy. What's yours?'

'Just Manxmouse.'

'Haven't you any first name?'

'No,' said Manxmouse, 'I don't think I have.'

Wendy held him off a little and said, 'Oh, then may I

call you Harrison? Harrison Manxmouse—don't you think that's a distinguished name? And will you be my friend?'

'I should like that very much,' Manxmouse replied, for of all the things that had happened to him since he could begin to remember, this seemed to be quite the nicest.

'Wendy Harrison Troy,' said the child, 'and Harrison Manxmouse. No, that isn't quite right. There's something missing. There ought to be another letter in there. I know —Harrison G. Manxmouse.'

'Yes, that is nicer,' said the Mouse, 'But what does the G. stand for?'

'Not anything. Just G. It makes it sound better. And afterwards, if you feel you need another name, you can invent one like I did, but beginning with 'G', like George or Gavin or Gregory.'

What a wonderful day this was turning out to be. From a plain ordinary Manx Mouse running away from a brown man with a broom, he was now Harrison G. Manxmouse and the friend of a little girl.

Wendy too, was enchanted and looked Harrison G. over from every angle. 'What a lovely colour you are. And what soft fur. I think it's such fun that you haven't a tail. And your ears are simply adorable. I'm going to kiss you.'

She did and Manxmouse thought that his heart would burst. No one had ever kissed him before. He cried, 'I think you're beautiful, too.'

'Honestly?' said Wendy, 'Nobody else does. They keep telling me my nose is too long and my mouth too big. And my eyes are supposed to be a funny colour, and I'm too tall for my age, and skinny. I'm ten. How old are you?'

'Not very,' replied Manxmouse, for he actually did not know, or rather could not remember.

'We'll be *best* friends, Harrison G. Manxmouse,' Wendy said, 'and have secrets together and not ever tell anyone and you'll stay with me always.' She held him to her soft cheek again and Manxmouse squeaked for joy.

Suddenly from a little distance away came the sound of a clock striking the quarter hour.

'Oh dear!' Wendy cried, 'We must hurry, or I shall be late for school. I'll put you in my pocket and there you'll be safe and nobody will know that you're there.'

She was wearing a blue school pinafore under her coat and gently deposited Manxmouse in the right hand pocket. 'Now we'll have to be quick,' and off she ran.

This was how Manxmouse, now Harrison G. Manxmouse, came to go to school with Wendy H. Troy.

The first lesson of the morning was arithmetic which was taught by a Miss Martinet and from the snug depth of the pocket, Manxmouse heard her say, 'Wendy, go to the blackboard and do this sum'. As she did so, the voice continued, 'Write this: A farmer had six bushels of corn, four bushels of rye and three bushels of wheat. The mice got into the barn and ate up two bushels of corn, one bushel of rye and half a bushel of wheat. How much grain did the farmer have left?'

As Wendy stared at the blackboard upon which she had written the problem (it was the half bushel that worried her, otherwise the answer would have been easy), she became aware suddenly of the most tremendous commotion in the right hand lower region of her pinafore.

Manxmouse was wriggling around in circles there
absolutely hysterical with delight and squeaking—'Nine
and a half! Nine and a half bushels! And a lot of happy
mice.' For if there was one kind of sum that Manxmouse
could do with his eyes shut it was naturally that one, being
a mouse himself. And he went on, 'Two from six is four;
one from four is three and half from three leaves two and
and a half. Four and three is seven, plus two and a half
makes nine and a half. Hurry up and write it.'

Wendy put her hand down to quiet him for it seemed
to her that the whole class must have heard him shout. But
it was too late.

'Wendy Troy,' came the voice of Miss Martinet, 'what
is that you have in your pocket?'

'N-nothing,' said Wendy.

The voice rose a level, 'Wendy! I distinctly saw something moving and heard a noise, like a squeak. You will
produce at once what you have in your pocket.'

There was no escape now. Wendy reached in and
brought out Manxmouse. For the first time he saw the
class of children seated at their desks, giggling and Miss
Martinet holding a ruler. She was long, thin, stern and
grey. 'What on earth have you there?' she said.

Wendy was not frightened, at least not yet, but only
sorry that her new and secret friend had been discovered
so soon. She was also cross with herself that she had not
been able immediately to work out such a simple sum. 'A
Manx Mouse,' she replied.

'A what?'

'My Manx Mouse,' Wendy repeated.

Miss Martinet lowered her spectacles onto the bridge

of her nose and peered over them to see better, and then said firmly, 'Don't talk nonsense child, there isn't any such thing.'

'But there is, truly,' protested Wendy.

Miss Martinet looked shocked and rapped on her desk with the ruler. 'Wendy,' she said, 'I'll take you to the office of the Principal at once, for telling a lie. And if it isn't a lie and there is such a thing, then you're to go for bringing it into the classroom with you. Right about turn —March!' And with Miss Martinet walking behind her, Wendy, holding Manxmouse cupped in her hand, went off to see the Principal who was short, thick and pink.

He looked up from writing at his desk as they entered and said in the voice reserved for such occasions, 'Ahum! And what is it we have here now?'

'This child,' Miss Martinet reported, 'came into my class with . . . with . . . this . . .'

'Manx Mouse,' Wendy concluded for her.

'Manx Mouse, indeed!' sniffed Miss Martinet. 'Obviously there can't be any such creature. You have only to look at it. This girl is always dreaming to herself and inventing things, but she oughtn't to be allowed to bring them into class with her.'

The Principal said, 'Er . . . put it down on my desk, my dear,' and Wendy did so. Manxmouse sat up looking a little sad. He hoped he had not got his friend into serious trouble by trying to help her.

As he leaned down for a closer examination, the Principal was heard to murmur, 'Hmmmmm,' and, 'Well, I must say,' and, 'No tail, and blue all over; those are kangaroo feet or I'm a donkey and whoever saw ears like that on any kind of mouse? Manx Mouse was what she said. It seems hardly likely. Still, with children one never can tell.'

Then aloud he said, 'Perhaps we'd better look into this a little more closely before pronouncing judgement.' He then pressed a switch on a small call box atop his desk and leaning his pink face to it, said, 'I want the history, the biology, the physiology, the chemistry and philosophy teachers to come to my office immediately.'

When they arrived somewhat breathless and wondering why they had been summoned, the Principal explained: 'I have asked you to come in order to give us the benefit of your learning. This child here claims that—er—what is supposed to be sitting on my desk is a—ah, what did you say you thought it was?'

'A Manx Mouse,' Wendy replied.

'There you are. You heard. And since there isn't any such animal, I should be pleased to have your opinions.'

All five then crowded around for examination, almost bumping their heads together as they produced spectacles, magnifying glasses and watchmaker's lenses from their pockets which they screwed into their eyes, studying Manxmouse fore and aft and from all angles.

The history teacher, a woman, was the first to give an opinion. 'It's a myth,' she said, for she also lectured on mythology. 'A mythical animal that existed only in the minds of people in ancient times, like the unicorn, the griffin, the dragon, the sphinx and the basilisk. But I've never seen a live one. It ought to be chloroformed, stuffed and put on exhibition in the classroom of the Lower Fourth.'

'Nonsense!' protested the biology instructor, 'It's

obviously some new and as yet unclassified species, of the Genus *Mus* of the family *Muridae*. Give it to me and I'll dissect it, examine its liver, count its vertebrae and . . .'

'Waste of time,' interrupted the chemistry professor. 'Analyse it, that's the thing. Let me have a bit of its fur and whiskers, some of its blood and maybe a toenail or two in my test tubes and I'll have the answer for you in a jiffy.'

'Faugh!' snorted the physiologist, 'You can't tell a thing until you examine its circulatory system and bone structure. Just give me a chance to inject it with dye, pickle it in alcohol, slice it into sections and put it under my microscope.'

The doctor of philosophy now became excited and shouted, 'No, no, no! It's much more simple than that. Logic is the way to tackle the problem. I'll give you an example. It's called a sillygism.' Here he put his finger to the side of his nose and recited:

'Nobody ever heard of a Manx Mouse.

In order to exist, somebody must have heard of it.

But I am somebody and have never heard of it.

Therefore the Manx Mouse does not exist.'

Everyone looked momentarily stupefied at this marvellous example of learning until Wendy said, 'But look! He's sitting right there on the desk.'

The philosopher appeared a bit taken aback at this but recovered immediately and said, 'Well, logic can't be wrong, so I vote we kill it and throw it out and then it won't be there.'

And now suddenly they all began to quarrel amongst themselves, each clamouring for possession of the Manx Mouse and milling around the Principal's desk shouting:

'Stuff him!' 'Cut him up!' 'Pickle him!' 'Deny him!' 'Inject him!' 'Slice him!' 'Analyse him!'

'Ladies and gentlemen!' cried the latter, 'Quiet please! I understand your zeal, but I must have time to consider which one of you is to have it, or maybe all of you just a piece of it. In the meantime he is to be put into a box under lock and key in the laboratory. I will give you my decision in the morning. Dismissed!'

They all trooped out except Wendy and Miss Martinet. Wendy begged. 'Oh please, can't I have my Manx Mouse back? I don't want him to be hurt or killed . . .'

'Too late. You should have thought of that in the first place,' the Principal said and then added, 'However, just think of the contribution you may be making to science.'

'Aren't you going to punish the child?' inquired the teacher.

'Yes, yes, of course,' replied the Principal rather absent-mindedly, for the Manx Mouse was now sitting up on his desk with a most touching expression of kindness combined with resignation on his face remarkable in one threatened with so horrible a fate. 'Have her write one hundred times: "I must not cause trouble to people by imagining things".'

And so with a heavy heart, Wendy went back to her classroom and after school stayed in for a long time writing her lines.

*   *   *   *   *

It was almost dusk when a certain Mr Mellow finished correcting his papers, locked up his desk in the school and prepared to go home.

Mr Mellow was the poetry teacher, a young man with flaming red hair, and friendly eyes.

As he went down the corridor he heard the sound of weeping and saw that it came from a little girl sitting alone in an empty classroom, her face buried in her arms.

He went in, and recognizing her, said, 'Why, Wendy, what on earth is the matter?'

She looked up and sobbed, 'Oh, Mr Mellow! They're going to do the most awful things to my poor Manx Mouse.'

'Oh, are they?' asked Mr Mellow, who, being a poet of sorts himself was never surprised at anything. 'Tell me about it.'

And thereupon Wendy did, from the very beginning. When she had finished, Mr Mellow said gravely and without questioning her story, 'Where did you say they had him?'

'In a box, locked away in the laboratory.'

Mr Mellow looked and listened. There seemed to be no one about. He whispered to Wendy, 'You come with me and we'll go and see. I might just have a key that could open the door. But tiptoes and don't make a sound.'

They crept upstairs to the second floor. And sure enough, the fifth key on Mr Mellow's ring worked. He switched on a shaded lamp and said, 'Come.'

On the long laboratory table was a small wooden box from inside of which came a frantic rustling, scrabbling and squeaking. And laid out on the table too, was everything prepared for whatever was to happen the following morning. There was a jar of spirit for preserving, test tubes, Bunsen burners and bottles of smelly chemicals for analysing. Also there were knives, scissors and scalpels for dissecting and vials of different coloured dyes for injec-

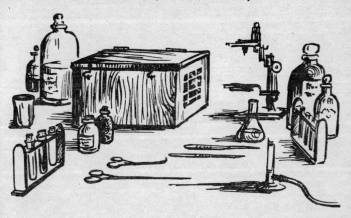

tion—all the terrifying tools of scientific exploration.

Mr Mellow went over and opened the lid of the box and they looked in as Manxmouse gave a shout of relief, 'Oh, Wendy! I knew you'd come.'

The poetry teacher said half to himself, 'Well, well! Then it's my dream too, now. What a dear little fellow.' He lifted him out gently and placed him in Wendy's hand, and she petted, kissed and cuddled him. Then being careful not to squash Harrison G., she threw her arms about Mr Mellow and cried:

'Oh thank you, thank you! You've saved him.'

'Shhhhhhh!' he whispered. 'We mustn't be caught now.' Putting out the light and locking the door, they hurried down the stairs and into the road that went past the schoolhouse. It had grown darker.

'What will you do with him now, Wendy?'

'Take him home.'

'Ought you not to let him go free?'

'Let him go? Why?'

There was a most curious expression on Mr Mellow's face and once more he seemed to be speaking half to himself. 'Because we are never allowed to keep our dearest dreams. There are always those who set out to destroy them. And besides, he belongs to Manx Cat.'

And then with a shock he realized what he had said. He did not know why he had said it, except that it seemed all to be a part of the strange happenings ever since he had heard a child crying by herself in a classroom.

'Oh, I *am* sorry,' he apologized.

'That's all right,' said Manxmouse. 'It's something that *everyone* says. And I suppose some day it will happen.'

'But I don't understand,' Wendy said, 'Why must I let him go? I love him.'

'Because he isn't a secret any more,' replied Mr Mellow. 'People know about him. They will come to you and find him and take him away again.' And then he added, 'You've had him and loved him, haven't you, Wendy? That is more than is given to many of us.'

Manxmouse said nothing, for this was beyond his understanding. Besides, he was wondering when and where and how he would finally meet Manx Cat and what his end would be.

Wendy looked up into the face of the poetry teacher saying, 'Would it be better for Manxmouse?'

'For both of you.'

They went down the road and then turned off into a lane close by some woods. Near the edge there was a copse of trees in a circle, almost like a fairy ring. 'Now this would be a likely place,' said Mr Mellow. 'He'll be quite safe here, even if they come looking for him. Then he can be on his way.'

Wendy held Manxmouse to her cheek and kissed him again. She said, 'Oh, I'm sorry, Harrison G. Manxmouse. They spoiled our secret. But at least you have a first name and a lovely initial now. Goodbye.'

'Goodbye, Wendy H. Troy,' said Manxmouse, and put his two strange kangaroo-like paws to her cheek, 'I'll always remember you.'

They left him sitting up watching them within the fairy ring of trees and Wendy turned her back quickly so that Manxmouse would not see that she was crying.

Mr Mellow reached down and took her hand, 'Come,' he said, 'I'll walk home with you.'

8

The Story of the Terrified Tiger

IT was a week later that Manxmouse met the tiger. The weather had changed almost immediately and as though to make up for past kindnesses, April came roaring back rather more like March with cold and rain and wind; wet grey days and miserable blustery nights. Whichever way Manxmouse travelled—north, east, south or west, it remained the same, chilling and soaking him until he thought he would never be warm again.

And as to how he travelled, sometimes it was on foot but more often by lorry. For Manxmouse had become quite clever at hitching rides for long distances without the drivers ever knowing he was there.

He would wait until one of them would stop, whereupon he would creep out from under a bush, climb up the left rear wheel and nip under the canvas at the back. There he would stay until he decided he had gone far enough. Sometimes there was even a meal to be had, for often the vehicles were loaded with fruits or goodies on their way to the big cities.

After one of these rides Manxmouse would climb down, wait until the lorry had departed and then walk along the road until he came to the nearest signpost, which would give him an idea of where he was.

On this occasion it appeared to be in the wilder part of Nevershire, near the town of Ringround, for he had caught a lorry going north carrying a consignment of Bakewell tarts of which he had treated himself to a rather large portion and did not wish to be caught by the driver. So when they had come to a halt, he had dropped off quickly and made his way westwards across country.

Before he had proceeded more than a few hundred yards he was soaked to the skin again, for it was a foul day, freezingly cold with the rain coming down in sheets. The drops driven by the wind were like bullets and hurt his tiny body. Manxmouse was forced to look for shelter. He found it in a thick copse of bushes, at the foot of a tangle of trees. And there he came upon the tiger.

For one terrible moment Manxmouse's heart stopped beating for he thought this must be Manx Cat and his end was at hand. It was certainly the largest cat he had ever seen, a thousand times bigger than himself, striped like a ginger and with eyes that glowed like the headlamps of the lorries Manxmouse had been riding. And at first glance and the shock of meeting in the confined space of the copse, it seemed to have no tail. It was only later that Manxmouse discovered that it was withdrawn between the legs.

At the same time that Manxmouse leaped back with a shriek of 'Manx Cat!', the tiger recoiled with a 'Who's there?' And then, upon seeing who and what, he crouched down again with a low moan and sighed, 'Oh, it's only a mouse. Imagine me, a tiger, being frightened by you!'

So it was not Manx Cat after all! Manxmouse felt he

103

could hardly say, 'It's only a tiger'. For all he knew, tigers were even more dangerous than Manx Cats were supposed to be and this one was so enormous that he could have swallowed Manxmouse at a gulp and never even felt him go down his throat. Yet he made no move to do so. On the contrary he seemed to be a most unhappy beast for he whimpered, 'Oh dear! What am I going to do?'

'Do?' repeated Manxmouse. 'What would a tiger be doing here anyway in the middle of England? Besides, I didn't know there were any tigers in England.'

'Well there is and I'm it. And what's more, I'm in a fix. You see, I've done the silliest thing. I've run away.'

Manxmouse came closer for obviously there was nothing now to alarm him. He said, 'Run away? From where and whom?'

'From my circus,' moaned the tiger. 'I must have been out of my mind. I don't know what came over me all of a sudden. But one of the new men left the door of my cage open and before I realized, I was through it and off.'

'But didn't anyone see you?' Manxmouse said. 'Aren't they looking for you?'

'Well, that's just it,' the tiger replied. 'Men will come and hunt me with guns and pitchforks and worst of all, my trainer will think I don't love him any more. No, no! There's nothing anyone can do for me.'

'I could try,' said the Manx Mouse. 'My name is Manxmouse, Harrison G.'

The tiger raised his head, 'My name is Khan—Burra Khan. It means Great Lord. I'm a fine Lord, aren't I? Take a look at me.'

Manxmouse did and had to admit to himself that he had never seen a drearier-looking specimen. The tiger's beautiful black, orange and white striped coat was soaked, matted with mud and full of burrs, nettles and leaves.

'It's this British weather,' said Burra Khan, 'not fit for beast or man. I've never been so wet and cold in my life before. It's all my own fault for not using my head. There was the open door and if I'd just stayed where I was, somebody would have come and closed it. But no, my curiosity again. I had to go through it to have a look-see at some of your country. Country! Ugh!'

Here he shook himself, sending a shower of spray and

mud flying in all directions. 'You can have it! No sun to dry one out; no good places to hide and nothing to eat. They must have broadcast an alarm about my escaping. I haven't come across so much as a dog at large.' Here he noticed that Manxmouse looked up at him a little nervously and moved a few inches away. 'You needn't worry, young fellow,' Burra Khan said, 'I don't eat Manx Mice. That's for . . .'

'I know,' said Manxmouse, just a little wearily, 'Manx Cat.'

'I didn't mean any offence,' Burra Khan said, 'I'm really glad to see you. I'm frightened. I just don't know what to do.'

'But were they cruel to you in the circus that you ran away?' Manxmouse asked.

'Oh my goodness, no!' replied Burra Khan. 'That's why I'm so angry with myself. I had a wonderful life. Two cracking good meals a day, a warm dry place to sleep no matter how hard it was raining or blowing outside. Even in the dead of winter I had a properly heated cage; a lot of friends to talk to and not much work. Twice a day in the ring doing a couple of silly tricks and that was it. The rest was money for jam.'

'But I thought that trainers were cruel, beat you with sticks, or long whips, used red hot pokers, or exploded pistols in your face to make you do what they wanted.'

Burra Khan gave a disdainful snort. 'Nobody tries that with us any more. That's out of date. My trainer works without saying a word. We understand one another. It's a job, see?'

'Not quite, I don't,' said Manxmouse.

'Well, look here,' Burra Khan explained, 'the circus pays my trainer and he looks after me. Now if he were to go pushing me about and making me irritable, or I were to mess him up—one claw would do it, you know—there wouldn't be any act, would there?'

'But wouldn't you like to be free?' Manxmouse asked.

'What, without my trainer?' Burra Khan answered. 'I should say not! He's my pal. He's just like another tiger to me. I'm much better off with the circus. Do you know how old I am?'

'I couldn't guess,' Manxmouse replied.

'Fourteen. And I've never been in better shape in my life. Do you know where I'd be if I were in the jungle today? Dead five years or more—food for the vultures.'

The tiger seemed to be staring back into the past. 'I've seen enough of jungle life: starvation, water holes drying up, white hunters looking for rugs. You get cut up in a bit of a battle and there's no one to look after you. The wound goes septic and that's the end of you. My trainer takes better care of me than he does of his own family. He rubs my head, scratches my tummy and hugs me. And when I get sick he gives me medicine and sits up with me all night. You show me any other tiger who would do that!'

'How can he be both a man and a tiger at the same time?' Manxmouse asked, bewildered by Burra Khan's story.

'Well,' said the big beast, 'it's a kind of game of pretend between us. He carries a long whip and a stick into the cage with him. I hit the stick with my paw, pretending I think that I am hitting him. The whip is just to give me my cue what to do. He never forces or makes me do anything I don't want. He *asks* me. And when I've done it, he says "Thank you!" '

'And I'll tell you something else; he doesn't really like to see me do silly things like sitting up and waving my paws, balancing on a barrel or jumping through a flaming hoop. Every so often he will come to my cage after the act and rub my ears and say, "Sorry, old fellow—but it's a living, isn't it?" How can you help but care for a chap like that? And now I've run away and caused him nothing but trouble. They've got out the police and the soldiers. If I frighten anyone, the circus will be sued. If I'm shot, he'll be out of a job.'

'Oh, I wish I could help you!' Manxmouse cried, for Burra Khan had painted a clear enough picture of the pickle into which he had got himself. Men with dogs and guns would soon be beating the countryside. Women and children must be trembling behind closed doors. Neither was a tiger on the loose a good thing for old people with bad hearts.

'What could you do?' moaned Burra Khan, 'It's my fault and this will be the end of me.'

'Oh, come on, now,' Manxmouse said, 'Tigers don't give up that easily. For one thing, I'm so small that nobody notices me. Do you know where the circus might be?'

'It's not far,' Burra Khan replied, 'I followed it during the night. There's a cliff a few hundred yards from here. The circus is just outside the town at the bottom of it. There'll be a big tent in a vacant lot somewhere, with smaller ones and painted wagons and cages all around. There'll be a horse tent and elephants staked out. You wouldn't be able to miss it.' And he named and described to him all the animals he would see.

'I'll go,' Manxmouse said eagerly. 'I might think of something. You stay here and don't stir. When I get an idea, I'll come back for you.'

'You're a good fellow,' Burra Khan said. 'I won't budge.'

Shortly after, hustling along in the direction that Burra Khan had indicated, Manxmouse found the show, or rather he almost fell into it.

For he had been making his way along a plateau of high ground, rough country of woods and rocks, when suddenly without warning he came to the edge of the cliff. Looking down he saw the circus at the bottom of it and nearby a small town.

It was exactly as Burra Khan had said: a large tent with a flag flying from its ridgepole and many smaller pennants fluttering, and strings of coloured electric lights. There were wagons about with cages attached, gaily-painted living wagons, a long tent in which he could see horses with shining jewel-studded harness and feather crests on their heads. And further down, staked out in the open, was a line of huge grey beasts that had a most familiar look. And then he remembered what Burra Khan had told him,

'Well, for goodness sake!' he said to himself, 'So an elephant is really a Nellyphant!'

He remained watching to see what else he could learn and at the very end of the row of beast cages in which he could see lions and leopards, wolves, monkeys and many other animals, he saw one that was empty with the door swinging open. That must have been the one from which poor Burra Khan had escaped. How to get him back in there with no one any the wiser? Manxmouse wished desperately to accomplish this, for it was so sad to see so huge and beautiful a creature as Burra Khan miserable, discouraged, frightened and hopeless.

And as he looked down from above, the tiger's plight was even more vividly borne home to Manxmouse. For a large group of people now emerged from the main tent, where apparently some kind of a meeting had been going on. Amongst them he saw policemen and soldiers, and roughly dressed men who were in all likelihood farmers and hunters. They carried guns and some had dogs of various kinds on leashes. It was evident that there would be no performance that evening, but instead renewal of the death hunt for the unfortunate tiger. Manxmouse saw a man sitting in front of the empty cage with his face bowed into his hands, and wondered whether this was Burra Khan's trainer.

From down below came the faint piping of a police whistle and the men split up into three groups: one went north, one south and one west. But none came towards where he lay hidden at the top of the cliff. Perhaps they had combed that area before, or having an insufficient force were planning to search in that direction later.

It was a great piece of good fortune. Manxmouse turned and scrambled as fast as he could back to the copse, but stopped short so as not to alarm the tiger further and squeaked, 'Burra Khan! It's me—Manxmouse! I'm back again.'

'But it's no use, is it?' said Burra Khan and his tone was hopeless.

'As a matter of fact, I have a sort of an idea. It mightn't

work, but it's worth having a go. If you could move very quietly . . .'

'That's my speciality!' said Burra Khan, and for the first time seemed to take heart. 'Do you really think . . .?'

'Let's have a try,' said Manxmouse, for he actually did have an idea at the back of his head and was dying to find out if it would work. 'But we must wait until it's dark. Then I'll lead the way. When I call, come along.'

They remained hidden until night had fallen. The wind had gone about and started up again, so had the rain which was a good thing, for it would keep people indoors. Both Manxmouse and Burra Khan had night vision and so this was no problem.

They progressed slowly but surely. Manxmouse would proceed for thirty or forty yards, then sit up, look, listen and then whisper, 'Come on!' A few seconds later, without having made a sound, the great bulk of Burra Khan would be alongside him.

In this manner they came to the edge of the cliff and peered down. The sight that met them was not encouraging. Although the circus was brightly illuminated with searchlights, no performance was being given for the news of the escaped tiger naturally had been in every newspaper and on radio and television as well. No one was going to risk going out until the beast had either been recaptured or shot. The search party with guns and dogs had returned and was standing about in front of the main tent, discussing the affair.

'Oh dear, oh dear!' moaned Burra Khan, and lay down with his face between his paws. Great tears rolled from his eyes as he looked upon his empty cage, the door standing open, the other wagons with all his friends. 'Oh dear, oh dear,' he repeated, 'it's hopeless.'

Manxmouse crept close and whispered, 'Come on, now Burra Khan! Buck up! Have a little courage.' And then he almost had to laugh at the idea of a Manx Mouse no more than two inches high, telling an enormous tiger to have courage. Yet for all his small size and defencelessness, when it came to doing something for others, there seemed to be nothing Manxmouse would not dare. He said, 'There's my plan. We could try it.'

'Your plan?' Burra Khan said, lifting his head. 'I'd forgotten that. What is it?'

'I'd rather not say,' said Manxmouse, 'in case it doesn't come off. Can you see whether there's any way down from this cliff?'

Burra Khan crept to the edge of the bluff and peered over. He said, 'Yes, there are some rocks jutting out and then a tree, and even what seems to be a footpath. Yes, I could make it, but I'd never get past the men with the guns. Can't you see that?'

'That's where my plan comes in,' said Manxmouse. 'I shall try to create a diversion.'

'You?' Burra Kahn questioned.

'I know I'm not very big or brave,' Manxmouse said, 'but stay here and wait and wish me luck. If the diversion should take place properly, come down as fast as you can and jump back into your cage.'

'How will I be able to tell?'

'You'll know,' said Manxmouse. 'Now, get yourself ready.' And he slipped off into the night, over the cliff, dropped onto the outcropping of rock and thence to the branch of the tree, gained the footpath and made his way down to the circus.

*   *   *   *   *

A mouse, particularly a Manx Mouse coloured blue, with no tail to be stepped on, can go practically anywhere at night without being seen. Manxmouse blended in perfectly with the dark shadows thrown by the bright circus lighting. He crept beneath the beast wagons and cages and avoided the main tent. He skirted where the horses were tethered and at last came to where six enormous Nellyphants, or elephants as Burra Khan had called them, were chained in a row by one hind leg and one fore leg. There they swayed, standing in straw some six inches deep, grumbling, muttering and phoophing to themselves, or picking up bunches of hay with their trunks and scattering it over their backs.

Manxmouse's plan for creating a diversion, by which he meant an uproar so that no one would notice the return of the unhappy tiger, was a simple one. It was based upon what he had learned from Nelly.

He certainly had not the slightest intention of running up inside the trunk of any of the elephants, but when it came to squeaks, rustles in the straw and tickling of feet, he felt that he could do a nice, competent job.

And so he slipped out of a patch of shadow and quick as a flash disappeared beneath the bedding close by the first elephant in the line.

She was peacably thinking elephant thoughts, when suddenly she stopped and her trunk stiffened. 'Hoo!' she cried, 'What was that? Oh, oh—I felt something.'

'What's the matter, dearie?' queried her husband who was swaying next to her.

'I don't want to say . . .' she said, 'but I think . . .' And suddenly she lifted her unchained foot high into the air with a shriek, 'Hoo! Oh! Ah! My foot! It's tickled!' And then raising her trunk on high, she trumpeted the alarm, 'Mowwwwwse!'

Immediately the other elephants took up the cry and the panic was on.

'Ooooh! Ouch! Help!'

'Mouse! I felt it! Police! Fire!'

'Haaaaaaalp! It's here now, under my feet!'

'No! I've got it! It's trying to run up my trunk!'

'Mouse! Mouse! Mouse! Call out the Army!'

'Ooooooh! It's going to crawl up my leg! I can't stand it! Hasn't anybody got a gun?'

'It's squeaking and rustling right under me now! Assistance! To the rescue, somebody!'

'Come on, boys and girls! Let's get out of here!'

And with that, lunging with all their strength, the elephants began to heave at the stakes that held their legs and the night was filled with the rattling of their chains, their shrieks and trumpetings and thumpetings. Manxmouse emerged from under the straw, at the other end of the line and sat up to watch the effect. It was far better than ever he had expected.

Beast men, roustabouts, trainers and performers came pouring out of their wagons at the racket. They were headed by the proprietor of the circus who was shouting, 'To the elephants, everybody! Something's got into them! If they break loose as well as the tiger, I'm ruined!'

Jingle-jangle! Clangety-clang! Bangety-bang! Smash-crash-bash! Wurroo-wurraa! Poom-Boom! Was there ever such a hullabaloo started up by one small mouse, and a Manx one to boot?

'Hurry, hurry!' shouted the proprietor, 'All of you with the guns get on over here too, but for Heaven's sake don't shoot! Just lend a hand. Bring ropes and chains. Where's that elephant man? Hang on to them! Don't let them get away!'

The job had been done. But would Burra Khan have had the courage to take advantage of it? Manxmouse ran around behind the milling, struggling group of elephants. Men were throwing nets over them, catching up their hind

feet with more ropes and chains. And Manxmouse was back at the empty cage of Burra Khan, just in time to see an orange and black streak flash by at such speed that the wind almost bowled him over, as the tiger sprang through the open door.

But so controlled was his body that he made not a sound as he landed on the floor. Once safely there, he whipped about, stuck out a huge paw, hooked two claws into the bars of the door and pulled. It clanged shut as the automatic catch clicked, and with a tremendous sigh of relief, Burra Khan flopped down crying, 'Made it! Manxmouse, old boy, you're the greatest! I never thought to see the day when I'd be rescued by a herd of looney elephants and a mouse, but it just goes to show that you never know. I won't forget what you've done for me.'

'Oh, it was nothing,' Manxmouse said modestly. I only hope I haven't made too much trouble . . .' and he looked anxiously over his shoulder in the direction of the hubbub.

'Oh, they'll manage,' said Burra Khan.

And indeed, the racket, hooting and uproar from the elephant pitch had already begun to die down as the circus men mastered the struggling beasts. The trainer, with admirable presence of mind, had swept their ground clear of straw and hay to show there wasn't a sign of any mouse there and that the whole thing had been imaginary.

Soon peace and quiet was entirely restored and the performers returned to their wagons once more.

A handsome, dark-haired young man clad in whipcord breeches, shiny leather boots and a white shirt which was soaked with perspiration, for he had been one of those who had worked the hardest to control the elephants, came walking slowly towards the cage. His shoulders slumped and he looked weary and despondent, his eyes cast down towards the ground.

Burra Khan made a strange, soft noise in his throat, whereupon the young man looked up and saw him. He gave a mighty and joyous shout, 'Burra Khan!' Then he ran to the cage, ripped open the door, hurled himself inside, and the next moment he and Burra Khan were hugging one another. The trainer, for of course that was who it was, rubbed the animal's head and pulled his ears, and the tiger purred and crooned over the man and licked his face and hands and Manxmouse was mightily pleased.

At that moment the proprietor appeared and saw what was happening, and he almost fainted.

'He came back!' the trainer cried to him, 'I knew he never really meant to leave me, did you, old fellow,' and he rubbed the tiger's head and hugged it hard to him, and Burra Khan just purred and purred.

Nor was the proprietor slow to take advantage of such good luck. 'Well, then,' he cried, 'we'll put on a show tonight. Send out a broadcast! Put it on the radio and the telly that the danger's over and the tiger's back. Get ready everybody!'

Immediately the circus lot was a-bustle with preparations, for it wouldn't take long to spread the news of the return of the tiger and curiosity to see him would bring out more people than ever. Manxmouse and Burra Khan were left alone for a moment, while the trainer went to dress and fetch a curry comb and brush.

Manxmouse said, 'Do you think I might stay and watch? I've never seen a circus.'

Burra Khan, now lay down with his head close to the bars of his safely locked cage and said softly with a strange air of tenderness in one ordinarily so fierce, 'Manxmouse, come closer. I want to talk to you.'

Manxmouse did so and sat up by the wagon where he could look into the glowing eyes of Burra Khan.

The tiger said, 'You know you've saved not only my life, but my happiness, and *his* happiness too,' and Manxmouse knew he meant the trainer he loved. 'There isn't anything I wouldn't do for you. But you cannot stay. I'd like you to be with us always, and travel with us. But if the proprietor ever found out you'd started the panic amongst the elephants, he'd never forgive you. An elephant stampede is a terrible thing. You'd be killed. You must go. Besides, there's your rendezvous with Manx Cat, isn't there?'

Manxmouse sighed. Must all his adventures, even the happiest ones, end on this note? Yet he did understand that the tiger was sending him away because he did not want him to be harmed by the circus people. He said, 'Well, perhaps I'll see a performance some other time, then. I'd better be going. Goodbye, Burra Khan.'

'Goodbye, Manxmouse.'

The mouse turned about and started off in the direction of the highway, when out of the darkness he heard the voice of Burra Khan calling, 'Manxmouse! Oh, Manxmouse . . .'

He stopped and called back, 'Yes, Burra Khan . . ?'

'Listen to me. You thought I was Manx Cat the first

time you saw me, didn't you?'

'Yes, I did,' Manxmouse admitted.

'But you weren't afraid.'

'Oh yes, I was.'

'But you didn't run.'

'Perhaps I was too scared.'

'I don't think so. I just wanted to say, Manxmouse, that you are braver than I am and if you aren't frightened, nothing can hurt you. Remember that.'

'Thank you, Burra Khan. I'll try.' Feeling strangely sad, the mouse continued on to the road where a lorry had just drawn up while the driver adjusted the ropes holding the canvas that had come loose on the far side. Manxmouse climbed up the inner wheel, entered and settled down to let it take him where it would.

9

The Story of the Greedy Pet Shop Proprietor

THIS time Manxmouse was not quite so fortunate in his choice of travel.

Actually it began most marvellously, when he discovered that his lorry was carrying boxes upon boxes of breakfast cereals.

There were so many different brands that he hardly knew where to begin. So he started at the top and ate down through Puffed Wheat, Cornflakes, Puffed Rice and All-Bran. Then he had some Sugar Puffs, which were delicious, followed by Rice Krispies and Weetabix. His exertions getting Burra Khan back into his cage had left him very hungry and so he gnawed his way through Honey Smacks, Grapenuts and Shredded Wheat, having a little of each and finishing with several other varieties with names ending in 'pop', 'snap' or 'crackle'.

By this time he was so full that he could hardly budge, and weary as well. So he curled up immediately and went to sleep.

But here was where the ill luck commenced. For the weather was still bad; the wind had been plucking at the canvas covering at the back of the lorry and now it was the other side that came loose and began to flap. The driver caught sight of it in his rear vision mirror, stopped and climbed down to secure it. And having stopped near a street lamp his eyes fell not only upon Manxmouse blissfully snoring, but on his trail down through the boxes.

The driver swore, then said, 'Well, you've been 'aving yerself a time, 'aven't yer?' He prepared to hit Manxmouse a bash that would have finished him off. But even as his fist was raised and he was about to bring it down, the light from the lamp glinted from Manxmouse's coat. The blow was halted in mid air while the man had a closer inspection and said, ''Ello! You're a funny-looking creature. I've never seen nuffink like you before.'

Manxmouse had eaten himself into such a stupor that he snored on. The driver picked him up in the palm of his hand and examined him from all angles. Manxmouse never budged.

'Might be able to flog 'im for a couple of bob,' the fellow said to himself. And so instead of crushing Manxmouse as he had planned, he slipped him into his pocket, firmly fastened the loose canvas, climbed back into his seat and drove off through the blustery night.

Manxmouse continued to sleep peacefully and happily all the way to London.

He woke when he heard voices.

''E's worth a quid if 'e's worth a penny. You ain't never seen one like that.'

'Go on! A quid for a mouse? I sell 'em for a shilling each. Give you sixpence.'

'Coo, guvnor, you ain't 'arf a sharp one! Sixpence for the likes of 'im? Wotcher got in here? Ordinary mice!

'Look at this little fella. Make it ten bob and you can 'ave 'im.'
It was daylight; they were indoors. Manxmouse was
being held in the palm of a horny hand and two faces were
bent over him, one a rough and rugged countenance, the
lorry driver. The other was a narrow one, with eyes set
somewhat too close together, topped by an almost completely bald head across which four remaining strands of
greasy dark hair had been laid.

Manxmouse became aware that he was in some kind of
a shop and that the faces were haggling over him.

'Give you two bob.'

'That you won't! I'd sooner knock 'im on the 'ead and
dump 'im into the river. Make it seven-and-six. 'E's ate
up arf the load orf me lorry.'

'Five bob and not a penny more.'

'It's a deal, guvnor!'

There was the chink of money. Manxmouse was trans-
ferred to another hand and almost immediately popped
into a cage and then he saw where he was and what had
happened. He had been sold to the proprietor of the Take
Me Home Pet Shop in Horsecollar Lane, London E.C.3.

Here there was every variety of small animal on sale
and the noise was deafening: the yapping and whining of
puppies, the mewing of kittens, the chirping of dozens
of birds, the squeaking of mice and squawking of parrots,
the chittering of guinea pigs, cooing of doves and the
chattering of monkeys. The only things that were silent
were the rabbits—white, brown and black Angora, and
goldfish cruising slowly about their tanks.

It seemed to be a well-stocked pet shop but Manxmouse

had yet to find out what kind of man the owner was.

For the proprietor, a Mr Smeater, was not exactly honest. His puppies which he advertized as pedigreed and which looked adorable whilst snoozing or wrestling in his window, invariably grew up to be yellow mongrels with huge feet and long, curly tails.

His Angora rabbits were ordinary plain ones dyed and his canaries were sparrows coloured orange. His goldfish were not gold, and his monkeys guaranteed as wonderful companions to a child, were nasty and bad tempered.

The kittens to which he gave fancy names were alley cats, and he paid a penny apiece for mice which he sold for a shilling. His parrots had never spoken a word in their lives and never would. When a customer came into the shop, Mr Smeater would switch on a tape recorder and immediately the parrots would appear to be saying, 'Hello, Polly! Pretty Polly! I like you. Polly wants a biscuit! Give us a kiss!' and other similarly absurd sentences that people seem to enjoy hearing parrots utter.

It might also be added here that Mr Smeater had a second tape recorder which, when turned on, made the fake canaries appear to be singing like mad things.

The guinea pigs which he sold as males were invariably females and shortly after leaving his shop were practically certain to produce a litter. When people complained, he would tell them they were lucky to get twelve guinea pigs for the price of one.

By these fraudulent means he had amassed a good deal of the only thing he cared about—money. Now, after the lorry driver had departed, he removed Manxmouse from his cage and holding him up by the nape of the neck said, 'Well, someone has certainly diddled you up and that's for sure.' For being a cheat himself, he simply could not imagine that such a creature as Manxmouse existed.

He moistened his finger, rubbed it along Manxmouse's fur and was surprised to see that no colour had come off. 'Hmmm! Good dye job,' he commented. 'But however did they get those ears stuck on?' And he pulled them until Manxmouse squeaked because it hurt. Then he turned him around and added, 'I can see where they cut off his tail—that was clever, but what about those feet? Well, whoever put this together certainly knew his stuff,' and popping Manxmouse back into the cage, he went into the back room for a moment.

Whereupon all the pets increased their racket, shouting and talking at once, and all querying simultaneously as to what Manxmouse might have been originally before someone had disguised him, as most of them had been tampered with.

'I'm a Manx Mouse,' said Manxmouse. 'And this is the way I am, honestly.'

All the animals except the mice began to hoot, shout and shriek with laughter, since they didn't believe him at all. The mice, on the other hand, made him welcome and hoped that he would be bought by a nice child who would look after him well.

At this point Mr Smeater returned carrying a sign which he had just lettered and which he hung from Manxmouse's cage. It read:

'TIBETAN TAILLESS LOP-EARED BLUE MINI-
    KANGAROO MOUSE. VERY RARE. 10/-

The mice were thrilled to have one of themselves, so to
speak, so expensive since they were the cheapest items in
the shop. But all the other animals thought that Manxmouse was ridiculously overpriced and would be giving
the other mice ideas, which indeed was the case.

It had all happened so quickly that he had not yet had a
chance to think or reflect upon the fix he was in, shut away
in a small box of a cage with a mesh front and up for sale
to goodness knows whom. At this point the bell over the
entrance door jangled, which was the signal for all the
pets to set up their racket again. A customer entered—a
gentleman with a small boy in tow.

Mr Smeater at once put on his most oily smirk and
advanced, rubbing his hands together. 'Good morning,
sir! Good morning, my little man! And what can I interest
you in today? A Burmese rabbit? They make very fine
pets. A sweet singing canary?' and here he secretly
switched on his canary recording. 'Or a Paradise monkey
from the island of Bali? A most unusual specimen—just
came in yesterday.'

Mr Smeater was a past master at inventing lies. The
monkey was an ordinary organ grinder's kind. He had
bought it the week before for a few shillings because the
organ grinder couldn't afford to feed it any more.

But the customer's eye seemed to be caught immediately
by Manxmouse, for he went over to the cage and after
examining him and reading the sign, said, 'Hmm, that's
certainly interesting. How would you like that one, Peter?'

'Oh, yes please, Dad!' replied his son.

The gentleman nodded in the direction of Manxmouse and said, 'Good. We'll have him then.'

'He's not for sale,' said Mr Smeater quickly. For he had been sharp enough to detect the gleam that had come into the father's eyes as he had examined the creature and at once the thought shot through his cunning mind. *Perhaps it is something very odd and I've priced him too low.*

'What do you mean, he's not for sale?' queried the customer. 'What's he up there for?'

'Just on exhibition.'

'Well then, why has he got a price—ten shillings?'

'That's not his price,' said Mr Smeater. 'That's his catalogue number—ten stroke dash.'

'Come on, now,' said the man, 'that's nonsense! What do you want for him?' And the more eager the customer was to buy Manxmouse, the more Mr Smeater was convinced that he might indeed have something rather rare and worth a great deal.

'He's a family pet. Belongs to my daughter.' (Mr Smeater had no family and certainly no daughter). 'We couldn't think of parting with him.'

'Well then, bother!' said the customer. 'Come on, Peter, we'll go somewhere else.'

Immediately he had left, Mr Smeater tore down the sign, rushed behind to his office again and made a new one, this time marking it '10 guineas'. He was certain the first person wouldn't have paid that, but somebody might.

At this juncture a white-haired gentleman arrived to buy food for his goldfish. He was an old client of Mr

Smeater's and a scientist who wrote fairy-tales for children when the things he discovered in science began to worry him too much.

He bought his box of fish food, paid for it and was just about to depart when he noticed Manxmouse. 'Hello,' he said, 'What have we got here?'

'What do you think of it?'

'Splendid little fellow,' said the old scientist, 'But of course, it isn't at all what that says it is. It's a Manx Mouse: *Musculus Lividus Sine Cauda*.' For scientists like to give long, Latin names to animals and all this one meant was, 'Little Blue Mouse Without a Tail.'

'Hmmm,' said Mr Smeater, 'It was sold to me as a Tibetan Miniature Kangaroo Mouse. But that just goes to show you can't trust anyone these days, doesn't it? Is it worth anything?'

'My dear man . . .' said the scientist, for he did not know that Mr Smeater was crooked and filled half his fish food boxes with sawdust, since his goldfish could not tell him. 'My dear man, worth anything? I think you may have hit upon something unusual. If it's genuine, as it seems to be, you may have the only specimen in existence. Well, I'll be getting along now. Two more of my fish died this morning. I can't imagine what can have got into them.'

Mr Smeater had a momentary twinge, since he knew what was getting into the scientist's goldfish, namely sawdust. But it was immediately overcome by his joy at having through some incredible stroke of luck, apparently hit upon something very valuable. As soon as his customer had left, he rushed into the back room, cooked up two new signs and attached them on Manxmouse's cage, where they caused a sensation. For one now read:
'BLUE TAILLESS MANX MOUSE. ONLY ONE IN EXISTENCE.' and the other: '20 GUINEAS.'

In a way Manxmouse was pleased at having been recognized by such a knowledgeable man, and by learning that there were no others like him.

The mice, of course, were quite hysterical with delight, since this had put up their standing tremendously. Indeed, Mr Smeater now raised the price of all the mice on the pretext of their being cousins to his Manx Mouse.

But the other animals were furious and kept shouting, 'Absurd!' 'Nonsense!' 'Ridiculous!' 'Twenty guineas for that silly-looking thing!' 'What's the world coming to?'

The scientist must have talked, shortly upon leaving the shop, for it was not long after that a rather breathless young man, wearing a badge which identified him as coming from the Zoo, rushed in and said, 'I hear you have a Manx Mouse. Ah, there he is! Twenty guineas—I'll have him,' and reached for his pocket.

This was too easy for Mr Smeater. If a man from the Zoo was willing to hand out twenty guineas without so much as a second look, the animal must obviously be worth a great deal more.

'Not so fast, my friend,' he said, 'it'll cost you fifty pounds.'

'What?' said the Zoo man. 'Fifty pounds? Why, you've got it written there—Twenty guineas. I'll pay you . . . ."

'Fifty pounds,' repeated Mr Smeater. 'That's not the price there. That just refers to the fact that I've twenty guinea pigs for sale. You know, twenty guineas, there they are over there in that window.'

'That's robbery!' said the Zoo man. 'I won't pay it.'

Before he could leave, another chap dashed in and spotting Manxmouse cried, 'Oh good! Then you haven't sold him yet. How much is he?'

The Zoo man said, 'He wants fifty quid for him.'

'Right you are,' said the second man, who was from the Museum, and produced his wallet.

'He couldn't have heard me right,' said Mr Smeater. 'I said a hundred.' For he was certain that if the Zoo would pay twenty guineas and the Museum fifty pounds, the Manx Mouse must be worth double.

The two went away disappointed, for neither could meet the new price set by Mr Smeater. Yet this was only the beginning.

It is surprising how, when there is something rare and unique in any field—in painting, sculpture, china or stamps and animals as well, the word gets around like magic and collectors appear from all sides, frantically competing to acquire the prize for themselves.

Soon Mr Smeater's shop was in an uproar as both men

and women, from various parks, laboratories, institutions, circuses and freak show proprietors attempted to buy the Manx Mouse. Each time the price was put up higher and higher, with Mr Smeater growing more and more excited with every new offer. Sometimes he would go faint as he thought how close he had come to refusing to give the lorry driver five bob for this treasure.

The mice by this time were in an absolute fever, while the other pets were too stunned even to make noises any more.

Naturally Mr Smeater no longer attached any price card to Manxmouse's cage, but merely quoted what he thought nobody could be so foolish as to pay and when they reached for their money, he at once raised the fee again. He knew such a treasure as this came into one's hands only once in a lifetime.

Even though greedy, he was on the point of closing a deal for a thousand pounds with an industrialist who had a private zoo. He could not imagine that anyone could possibly offer more for such an ugly little thing, when the door burst open and a messenger appeared with a fist full of telegrams.

The first one he opened was from Australia and said, 'AM FLYING LONDON DONT SELL MANX MOUSE UNTIL MY ARRIVAL WILL OFFER FIVE HUNDRED POUNDS MORE THAN ANYONE ELSE', and it was signed, 'J. W. WOOLMAN.'

The next, from South Africa read, 'ARRIVING LONDON TOMORROW 1900 HOURS HOLD MANX MOUSE FOR HIGHEST BID. P. G. DIAMOND.'

A third was from an oil magnate in Texas, another from a millionaire in New York and so it went.

Mr Smeater now saw riches beyond his wildest dreams: retirement, purchase of a large Rolls Royce, an eighteen-roomed house, travel, caviar and champagne every night. But how to be certain that he had been able to squeeze every last penny out of Manxmouse's value? How to be absolutely one hundred per cent sure that he had obtained the top price and that there was not someone who would give more?

Then in a blinding brainwave the idea came to him: put up the Manx Mouse for auction. Let them come then, one and all, the collectors, the crazy millionaires and fight it out amongst themselves. Thereupon, logically, the name of the greatest auction house in London, Bidemup's of Bond Street, entered his head.

To the crowd now milling about in his shop shouting and waving money at him, he said, 'Sorry gentlemen, the Manx Mouse is not for sale at the moment. I have decided to put him up for auction at Bidemup's, where you will be able to attend. I want to be fair to everybody.'

For not long before there had been a great to-do in the press over a painting by a Mr Fricasseo which had fetched the fantastic sum of £190,000. If some daubs with paint on a bit of canvas could fetch such a price, what a fabulous amount could be realized for the only existing specimen of a genuine Manx Mouse!

However, Mr Bidemup, the owner of the firm, was not at all pleased with either Mr Smeater's idea or Mr Smeater, when the latter first presented himself at his office with the Manx Mouse in his box cage under his arm.

Mr Bidemup was a very dignified gentleman with a black ribbon attached to his eyeglasses. He was wearing a most expensive suit of clothes, the kind Mr Smeater hoped to buy by the dozen after he had sold Manxmouse.

He looked at Mr Smeater most severely as he said, 'My dear sir, our establishment doesn't sell livestock. We auction valuable paintings, sculpture, china, old silver and jewellery. But animals? . . . And a mouse? Really, my good man, I suggest you take it to Petticoat Lane, or perhaps some pet shop will give you a few shillings for it.'

Mr Smeater, however, was not to be put off, since he had already had evidence of its value. He said, 'I don't think you realize, sir. This is hardly an ordinary mouse.' Here he opened the box and took out Manxmouse who sat in the palm of his hand and regarded Mr Bidemup with that mixture of gentleness, affection and tenderness which was always a part of his expression.

The auctioneer was startled to say the least. In the first place he had never seen such a delightfully pleasing and heart-warming look on the face of any animal before, and in the second, he had never seen any such animal. 'Hmmm,' he said, 'What is it?'

'A Manx Mouse,' said Mr Smeater, 'the only one in existence.'

'Charming little fellow,' said Mr Bidemup. 'How did you come upon him?'

'An expedition into darkest Borneo, the country of the

head hunters,' Mr Smeater began. 'After suffering untold privations . . .'

'Yes, yes! I see,' said Mr Bidemup, not believing a word of it. But the Manx Mouse somehow was exerting a spell over him. Yet rules were rules and he sighed and began to say, 'I regret . . .' when Mr Smeater played his trump card.

He took the cablegrams from his pocket and laid them on the desk before Mr Bidemup, who read each one quite carefully, after which he cleared his throat and said, 'Hmmm, well now, it doesn't do to be too rigid these days, does it? It so happens that next week we are having a sale of small porcelain figures— Dresden, Copenhagen, Staffordshire, Rosenthal, Meissen . . .' 'Aha!' said Mr Smeater, 'Well, if you're selling Mice-en whatever . . .' for he had no idea of the names of porcelain or how to spell their makers.

'Exactly what I was going to say,' concluded the Director. 'We might include your Manx Mouse under the heading of Meissen. However,' and here he cleared his throat again and waggled his glasses at the end of their ribbon at Mr Smeater, 'you understand that you must pay ten per cent of the final sale bid, whatever happens. Is that clear?'

'By all means,' answered Mr Smeater, so thrilled at his success he was hardly listening.

'And Bidemup's can accept no responsibility for the animal, his state of health, or delivery of same.'

'Yes, yes, of course!' Mr Smeater replied, only too delighted with the result of the interview.

'You'd better read the entire contract carefully, including the part in fine print,' warned Mr Bidemup.

'No, no, not at all necessary,' Smeater replied. He signed all the papers presented to him without even glancing at them and went back to his shop well satisfied with himself. He was about to become a rich man.

And so with the appearance of Manxmouse in Bidemup's catalogue and advertisements, he very quickly became a celebrity and Mr Smeater already began to take in money hand over fist. On the strength of the excitement he sold out almost all his stock, raising his prices and taking a pound a piece for his mice.

He charged the press photographers a fee for taking Manxmouse's picture and the newspapers another for publishing it. He collected a good-sized sum from the B.B.C. for letting Manxmouse appear on television and a further large amount by permitting him to be modelled in wax and exhibited at Madame Tussaud's.

He made even more money by clearing his shop and charging five shillings admission—children under ten, half-a-crown—to see Manxmouse, so that he already amassed a small fortune before ever the auction took place.

In the meantime almost every plane that touched down at London airport discharged prospective purchasers from foreign parts, loaded with money and hopes.

SEE THE UNIQUE MANXMOUSE
ADULTS 5/-
CHILDREN 2/6 ONLY ONE IN EXISTENCE

10

The Story of the Marvellous
Manx Mouse Auction

AN auction at Bidemup's, particularly when something of great value is to be put up, is a most exciting affair. The saleroom has chairs placed in rows somewhat like a theatre and the auctioneer operates from a pulpit like that in a church. Attendants bring in the objects to be sold and place them upon a raised pedestal where all can see. The auctioneer describes each one briefly and the bidding begins, sometimes running like wildfire around the room, at others settling down to a duel between two people who cannot even be seen, but who convey their bids by mysterious signals.

Nor is this all. To accommodate the many who wish to attend, other salerooms off the main one are equipped with closed-circuit television sets and a member of the firm transmits any offers made by telephone to the chief auctioneer.

But for the Great Manx Mouse Auction, as it came to be known in later days, there was even a further novelty. Transatlantic television via Telstar was arranged, so that those who could not manage to fly over, could bid via radio 'phone from such distant places as New York, San Francisco, Buenos Aires in the Argentine, and Sydney, Australia.

On the day of the auction, a Friday morning, every important person in London had used his or her influence to gain a ticket of admission and a seat at the sale. There were Baronets, Viscounts, Earls, even a Duke, along with stars of stage and screen, owners of diamond and gold mines, property tycoons, two deposed Kings and several Middle Eastern Sheiks who did not know what a Manx Mouse was, but if it was all that valuable thought they ought to own it.

For the great day Mr Smeater wore a tailor-made suit as expensive as that which he had seen upon Mr Bidemup but somehow on him it managed to look like all his others. As the owner of the Manx Mouse, he had a seat in the very front row.

The rooms were packed to suffocation by eleven o'clock when the auction began. Manxmouse was Lot No. 87, for the auctioneers always like to warm up the public to a pitch of excitement before bringing out the star item of the day. Moving picture, television and still camera men waited nervously beside their apparatus for the great moment that was to come.

As each succeeding lot was knocked down, anticipation mounted. In his little box cage under the care of one of the uniformed attendants, Manxmouse awaited his fate in considerable confusion.

He had never quite understood the whole affair, except that his 'owner', Mr Smeater, was not a very nice man what with his dyed birds and fish and cheating parrots. But he had had little time to reflect, it had all gone so rapidly. And now he was part of something called an auction.

As Lot No. 84 was sold, the crowd began to move uneasily in its seats. At No. 85, there was a shuffling of feet and a clearing of throats. At No. 86, women clutched the arms of their escorts to avoid fainting from the tension. At last Mr Bidemup placed his glasses at the end of their black ribbon upon the bridge of his nose and announced, 'Lot No. 87: One blue, tailless, Manx Mouse reputed to be the only one in existence.' The attendant gently lifted Manxmouse out of his box and placed him upon the pedestal where all could see. There was a great rustle and a murmur ran through the bidders. Necks were craned and people stood up to see amidst loud cries of, 'Down in front! Keep your seats, please!'

'I have a bid for fifty thousand pounds,' said Mr Bidemup, but immediately changed it to, 'One hundred thousand,' as someone must have signalled. 'A hundred and fifty thousand—Two hundred thousand—Two hundred and fifty—Three hundred . . . .

Manxmouse on his pedestal looked over the assemblage and wondered how it was that so many obviously good people in beautiful clothes could appear so flushed with greed. What on earth was it they wanted that made their faces so red, their eyes narrowed and their mouths all twisted and peculiar?

Mr Bidemup was wonderful. He never grew flustered or lost his head as the bidding mounted. 'Three hundred and fifty thousand,' he said, '. . . against you, Your Grace.

Four hundred thousand from New York. Four hundred and fifty from Buenos Aires. Was that you bidding, Your Majesty? Sorry, I couldn't see. Thank you, I have your bid, five hundred thousand . . .'

Half a million pounds! The excitement in the saleroom became almost unbearable.

'Five hundred and fifty thousand from San Francisco . . . Six hundred thousand, thank you Sheik Ibn-Cascarah . . . Six hundred and fifty thousand, at the back of the room.'

Mr Smeater hugged himself. Every time that somebody held up a hand or waggled a catalogue, or an electric impulse arrived from the other side of the world, he was fifty thousand pounds richer. Could it be possible that he was about to become a millionaire? Everyone in the auction room was asking themselves the same question as the price continued up to seven hundred thousand, seven hundred and fifty, and eight hundred thousand pounds.

At eight hundred and fifty thousand, the auction slowed down momentarily as they always do. People needed to catch their breath and consult their bank balances, and their consciences. And, sitting up on his pedestal with his gentle expression, Manxmouse was consulting his own. For at last understanding of what was going on had come to him and he was saying to himself, 'But this is ridiculous! Someone is going to spend all that money on me? I could never allow that. I'm not worth it. I'd never be able to have another peaceful night's sleep if I thought I'd let somebody pay that much money. And besides,' and here his face became somewhat sadder, 'I don't belong to Mr Smeater at all. I belong to Manx Cat . . . everyone has said so.'

'Are you all finished at eight hundred and fifty thousand pounds?' asked the auctioneer, and glanced about the gathering. And at this point an attendant crossed in front of the pedestal where Manxmouse was perched and whispered something to Mr Bidemup, who immediately announced, 'I have nine hundred thousand pounds. Sorry! Against you again, Your Grace. At nine hundred thousand . . . thank you, nine hundred and fifty thousand . . .'

And now as the fantastic figure of a million pounds was approached, the tension in the saleroom reached explosive proportions. Men loosened their collars, women fanned themselves.

Mr Bidemup intoned, 'Nine hundred and fifty thousand pounds, I am bid,' and he looked about the assembly and continued, 'Will anyone say a million?' For a moment you could have heard a feather drop. And then with a triumphant note in his voice, he announced, 'One million pounds is bid! At one million pounds—At one million pounds—Are you all done, then?' and with a sharp rap, his hammer fell and he announced, 'Sold to Sheik Ibn-Cascarah, at one million pounds.'

For, of course, sitting on half the oil of Arabia the Sheik had more money than anyone else in the world.

A great shout went up from the audience and a tremendous burst of applause, as the Sheik clad in his white robes arose to accept congratulations. Every lens was focused upon him.

Mr Smeater was jumping up and down with joy, saying to himself over and over, 'I'm a millionaire! I'm a millionaire!'

Such a sensational and dramatic moment had never

before been seen in the famous saleroom. That is, until the
attendant who had Manxmouse's box under his arm went
over and whispered something to Mr Bidemup, who at
first turned pale and then quite red. Beating upon his
desk with his hammer insistently until he had produced
quiet, he said, 'Ladies and gentlemen, have any of you seen
the Manx Mouse?'

There was a chorus of 'What? Where?' and all eyes were
turned upon the pedestal. It was empty. Manxmouse was
no longer there.

There was a gasp from the crowd and one could almost
hear it echoed from Sydney, Buenos Aires, San Francisco
and New York. A moment before the mouse had been
there; now it was not.

Sheik Ibn-Cascarah, already
dark of colour, was looking
even darker.

The auctioneer retained his
calm. He said, 'Naturally,
if the purchase cannot be
delivered, your bid is cancelled.
But perhaps he has got onto the
floor somewhere . . . Would
you all please have a look?'

And at that, although he
meant it for the best, the balloon
went up. A woman's voice was
heard to shriek, 'What, a
mouse loose on the floor? Help!'
and she got up onto her
chair.

Immediately the other women climbed onto the nearest ones, trying to pull their mini-skirts down over their knees and screaming. Other chairs were being overturned or were collapsing as the men and attendants searched under them. Clothing was torn, fist fights started and not until it became quite clear that there was no Manx Mouse anywhere did the confusion cease.

And naturally, he was not to be found, for at the moment that the attendant had crossed over in front of him, he had slid down the pillar of the pedestal, run under the seats to the rear of the room where the exit was, nipped across the floor, whipped through the hall, dashed down the stairs and out into the street. There, just at that moment, luckily, a cab drew up to the kerb and discharged a gentleman in a bowler hat carrying a briefcase and a rolled umbrella. As he paid the driver, Manxmouse leapt inside; the door was shut and the cab drove off with him.

And thus did the great, million-pound, Manx Mouse auction come to an end, except for a very unhappy session that Mr Smeater had with the head of the famous firm in his office, a little later. There, Mr Bidemup was saying, 'One million pounds at our usual ten per cent . . . that will be one hundred thousand pounds.'

'But the mouse has gone,' complained Mr Smeater. 'There wasn't any sale.'

As always, Mr Bidemup retained his stately cool. 'If you will remember, sir, the agreement was that you must pay a percentage of the final sale bid. If you will look there in the fine print . . .'

'But it's your fault!' screamed Mr Smeater, 'Your men

let the Manx Mouse go!'

'Paragraph 2, just below . . . where it says, "and Bidem-up's can accept no responsibility of any kind for the animal" . . . and, ahem, this is your signature at the bottom of the document, is it not?'

And there it was. Mr Smeater was compelled to pay over every penny of the money he had earned from Manx-mouse prior to the sale and sell his shop and his house to boot, to make up the difference. For his pains he was left only with the expensive suit of clothes which, as has been regrettably noted, did not make him look any better than had his old one.

As for Manxmouse, he was on his way somewhere in an empty taxi in London.

*   *   *   *   *

But the taxi did not remain empty for long. Even before it had reached Piccadilly it was hailed and a gentleman who looked exactly like the one who had got out, bowler hat and all, got in. 'Savoy', he said, and off they went.

Manxmouse squeezed himself into a corner on the floor where he would not be likely to be noticed. The cab twisted this way and that through the traffic until they drew up at the famous Savoy Hotel in the Strand, where the doorman said to the driver as the gentleman stepped out, 'Haven't seen anything of a Manx Mouse, have you? It's got away. Just heard it on the radio. Worth a million pounds.'

'Wouldn't know one if I saw one,' said the driver.

'Shocking looking thing,' said the doorman, 'About a foot high, they say, with horns and a stinger, and green

all over. Haven't left anything in the cab, have you sir?'
This to the passenger who was paying. And as they always
do, the doorman had a look for parcels, bags or umbrellas
forgotten.

Manxmouse squdged down as small as he could.

The doorman, however, was looking for something
quite different—people never manage to get things right
that they hear—and so did not see him, 'Yes, Madam,
Taxi . . .'

'Fortnum and Mason, please.'

When they arrived there it turned out to be London's
celebrated food shop with the most delicious-looking
hams, tongues, chickens, cheeses, jars of caviar, bottles of
fruits and wines in the window which started up Manxmouse's appetite again. But he did not dare get out, for
there was a commissionaire in an imposing uniform who
asked the driver the same question about the missing Manx
Mouse, and then said, 'You wouldn't hardly be able to
miss 'im. They say he's three feet long, with teeth like a
shark, purple scales and barks like a dog. Yes sir. Taxi.
Here you are, sir.'

This time an elderly gentleman got in and said, 'Ham-
ley's in Regent Street,' for he was going to buy a present
for the birthday of his niece. Hamleys turned out to be
one of the biggest and most marvellous toy shops in the
world and when they got there, it seemed, according to
the attendant who opened the door of the cab, that Manxmouse had grown wings like a bat, legs like a stork, the
hide of a rhinoceros and grunted like a pig.

'Marks and Spencer!' directed the next customer and
by the time they arrived at yet another well-known store,

Manxmouse was supposed to be about the size of a medium hippopotamus with a beak like an eagle's, tusks and hide like a walrus, the tail of a gibbon and the cry of a mother auk.

That was bad enough, but the feeling of being hunted was even worse. Everyone was looking for him or talking about him, and on a newspaper vendor's board outside Marks and Spencer, Manxmouse caught a glimpse of a bulletin scribbled in large letters: 'MILLION POUND BIDEMUP ESCAPE! ALL LONDON SEEKS MANX MOUSE!' People were crowding around and buying the afternoon papers at a tremendous rate.

By this time, Manxmouse had gnawed himself a small hole in the leather of the seat down by the floor and slipped inside whence he could peer out and see, but not be seen. And for the rest of the afternoon he was a part of what a London taxi driver lives through every day of his life; the frustrating stalls in traffic and never knowing where he will be bound for next.

They had calls to addresses in Harley Street, where all the doctors had their offices, fashionable Belgravia and arty Bloomsbury, to the Portobello Road, the British Museum and St Paul's Cathedral. They ranged as far north as Hampstead Heath and south to Battersea Rise. Manxmouse smelt that they kept passing the most wonderful green patches where he might have found a hiding place, such as St James's, Green, Hyde and Regent's Parks, but they never stopped at any.

When a passenger ordered the driver to take him to St Martin-in-the-Fields, Manxmouse took heart. Once in a field again he would feel safe. But the address turned out to be the name of a church in the heart of the busy city, by Trafalgar Square with not so much as a blade of grass in sight.

The fares were as diverse as the addresses, men, women, children, young, old, middle-aged, sick, well, chatty and silent. There were elegant ladies who sat up in prim-mouthed dignity, or more poorly clad working women who could not resist a natter with the driver, chiefly on the subject of the missing Manx Mouse who had now grown to the proportions of a beast the size of an elephant with a hump on its back, headlamps for eyes, a forked tongue and ten claws on each foot.

The cab picked up doctors, solicitors, clergymen, an actress on the way to rehearsal, a blind beggar who was not blind at all, but was moving his pitch from one part of town to another, and five hippies from Chelsea who were going to the Iranian Embassy to protest over something. They plucked on guitars and smelled bad.

An unexpected break came when the driver picked up a family outside Earls Court, London's big Exhibition Hall where there was a Dairy Show going on. They climbed into the taxi clutching handfuls of samples they had collected inside; cheeses, butter, powdered and malted milks and other edible products. When one of these fell to the floor of the cab, quick as a flash Manxmouse whipped it into his hiding place. While they searched for it, remarking that they could not imagine where it had got to, he had a satisfactory meal and felt better prepared to face whatever lay before him.

The weather had changed again, with intermittent rain and sunshine and now as it grew dark, Manxmouse knew that it was time for him to have a go at getting away. He could not remain in the cab for ever and the driver would soon be going home. But how? Leap out when the door was opened? With all London on the alert for *some* kind of a strange looking animal worth an absolute fortune?

It was shortly before six o'clock that the opportunity came. Another gentleman in bowler hat with umbrella and briefcase (London seemed to be full of them), hailed the cab just outside Buckingham Palace, where the Queen lived, giving Manxmouse a glimpse of it as he got in and said, 'Go to that newsreel cinema in the Marylebone road, near the Planetarium. I've an hour yet before my train.'

'Right you are, guv'nor.'

And Manxmouse saw that for once, his umbrella was not rolled, since it had been raining shortly before. Its owner leaned it against the seat. As they turned a corner it fell to the floor and by the time he had picked it up again, Manxmouse was inside it. In this way no one would see him leave the cab. What he would do thereafter would remain to be seen.

But he had not reckoned upon those treacherous skies. As they drew up at the cinema, the heavens decided to let go again.

The gentleman jumped out, said, 'Half a moment,' to the driver and opened his umbrella before reaching into his pocket for the fare. And out onto the pavement dropped Manxmouse.

It was hard to tell who was the more astonished. ''Ullo, 'ullo,' said the cabby, 'Where'd you pick '*im* up?'

'I can't imagine. It must have been in your taxi.'

'Garn! I ain't never 'ad a mouse in me cab in me life.'

And then suddenly staring, he cried, 'Lookee here, guv'nor, that wouldn't be that there Minxmanx they've been talking about? Grab 'im, guv'!"

'By Jove!' said the gentleman and bent over to do so. But Manxmouse was off and running hard with the man and the driver, who had jumped down off his cab, in

pursuit, the latter shouting, 'It's the Mooseminx! Stop 'im!'

But by now it was nearly dark and raining heavily. The streets were slippery, other pedestrians took up the cry and the chase, but they interfered with one another, or skidded. Since none of them knew exactly what they were chasing, this gave Manxmouse his chance.

On the right there seemed to be a building the entrance to which was ablaze with lights and there was a large sign over the door. Just at that moment all the lights went out leaving the front in darkness, but the door was still open with one or two stragglers emerging therefrom. Manxmouse did a beautiful right turn and dashed inside just as a man in uniform approached, dangling a bunch of keys.

He turned and shouted up a flight of stairs to someone, 'Any left, Joe?' to which the reply came down, 'All clear. What about 'Orrors?' From below another voice said, 'Ain't none down 'ere.'

'Okay, then,' said the attendant with the keys, 'Last one is out.' He pushed the heavy door shut and locked it just as the hue and cry behind Manxmouse came charging up. Manxmouse himself had ducked beneath a counter just inside and was keeping very still.

There came a pounding on the door from without and cries of 'The Manx Mouse! The Manx Mouse! Let us in!'

'Closed for the night!' the attendant shouted back.

There were more bangings and calls. 'The Manx Mouse! He's inside. Let us in.'

'Of course he's in here,' said the attendant. 'And no extra charge to see 'im. But you'll have to wait until tomorrow morning. We're closed now. Can't you read? It's six o'clock. Doors open at nine in the morning.'

Some still kept at it, crying, 'Open up! We know he's in there.'

The attendant laughed, 'So do we,' he said. 'Nine o'clock tomorrow and you can all come in at seven and six each, 'Orrors included.'

Eventually the pursuers became disgusted and went away. Four other attendants now appeared from various parts of the building. 'All the daft ones ain't in the looney bin,' said the chief with the keys. 'Can you imagine bein' all that crazy to have a dekko at a bloomin' mouse? Right then, goodnight Tom. See you tomorrow, Bill. Take the side door, Jerry. You goin' my way, Alf? What about a quick one?'

And the five left to change into their street clothes and go home. Manxmouse heard their voices once more as they left by the side exit. Then that door slammed and the key rattled in the lock.

Manxmouse crept out from beneath the counter. A few lights had been left burning. He was all alone but he had no idea where. And he was most puzzled by the behaviour of the men in uniform. For he had heard them admit to the pursuers outside that they knew he was there inside with them, and then refuse to let them in. They had instituted no search themselves but had told the ones outside to return at nine in the morning. It was most mysterious, baffling and confusing.

He had, of course, not the faintest notion, at least not at that moment, that he had found shelter and respite for the night inside Madame Tussaud's famous Waxworks Museum in the Marylebone Road. Here were on exhibition models not only of British heroes but famous and infamous people from all over the world.

11

The Story of Manxmouse meets Manxmouse

Now that he was alone and safely locked in, at least until the next morning, Manxmouse felt the best place for him would be down in the basement, which he thought would be rather a cellary place where he could hide. He had not understood the attendant's mention of the ''Orrors' and nobody being left down there, as referring to the famous Chamber of Horrors. This was the exhibit people went to see for the pleasure of being frightened out of their wits, and especially children.

But he soon found out. For with hardly any lights it was much more gloomy and terrifying. Nevertheless, Manxmouse could not resist a glimpse and a shiver at the reproduction of the mediaeval torture chamber, the guillotine, Mr Crippen, Jack the Ripper and various other murderers in their cells, and the original bathtub in which Charlotte Corday stabbed Marat during the French Revolution. However, it was not long before the presentation of ''Orrors' which included gibbets, racks, thumbscrews, pincers and assorted weapons used to commit particularly gooey murders, proved too much for Manxmouse and he ran shuddering up the stairs and then another flight to the first floor. In his hurry he never noticed the policeman standing on the landing.

He found himself in a very strange set of rooms indeed, where all the famous characters of history, ancient and modern, were collected. They stood about on platforms dressed in their proper costumes, but not saying a word.

True, there was nothing to be frightened of here. On the contrary it was something of an education to wile away the time. Manxmouse went about reading the signs at their feet.

There were Napoleon and Josephine, Mr Gladstone, Mr Lloyd George, and Mr Macmillan and Disraeli, former Prime Ministers, along with Queen Victoria and Queen Elizabeth I in a huge ruff and trailing gown. He saw Kings and Queens of Europe, Presidents of the United States, Jack Hobbs the cricketer and Stanley Matthews the football player. There were Sir Gordon Richards the jockey, Graham Hill the racing driver, and Sir Francis Chichester who had just sailed around the world all by himself, not to mention Hitler and Gamal Abdel Nasser, Stalin, Kruschev and a number of other international troublemakers.

In addition he came across a highly interesting panorama of Snow White and the Seven Dwarfs, Puss in Boots, Jack the Giant Killer and the Sleeping Beauty who lay in her bed as natural as life, for her breast moved gently up and down. Manxmouse stayed for quite a while gazing at her, marvelling. He did not know that she had some machinery inside her chest that made it move as though she were

breathing.
He went on to visit Guy Fawkes, Henry VIII and all his wives, Shakespeare, Lord Nelson, Wellington, Richard the Lionhearted and Sir Winston Churchill, when he suddenly came upon a sign with an arrow which read: 'SPECIAL ATTRACTION. This Way', and then in brackets, 'No Extra Charge'. He followed the direction and passed down to a small enclosure off the main hall. It was a circular room entirely surrounded by red velvet hangings. There was a rope stretched across the entrance to keep people out. The attendant had apparently forgotten to switch off some electricity and machinery, for there were several spotlights placed around the ceiling at various angles and they all shone down upon a slowly revolving pedestal set up in

153

the centre of the room. And on the pedestal, sitting up, Manxmouse saw—HIMSELF!

He had never had such a shock in his life!

There he was, the fat little body like an opossum's, the hind feet like those of a kangaroo, the front paws of a monkey and the long ears of a rabbit. There was no mistaking the identity for he was blue all over. The rabbit's ears were orange-coloured on the inside. And to make it binding, finally there was no tail, only the button where it ought to have begun. It was the perfect copy of himself in wax.

Imagine what it would be like if, walking in the street, you turned a corner suddenly and saw yourself coming towards you, and you could walk around yourself and see yourself as others see you, and from all sides.

This was now the experience of Manxmouse. And as if it was needed, at the base of the pedestal was the sign, 'THE MILLION-POUND MANX MOUSE. Only Specimen in the World.' For naturally, since the management had heard the news of the fabulous sale on the radio, it had quickly put up a new placard.

'W-who are y-you?' Manxmouse asked, thoroughly upset, not expecting an answer from a wax figure.

At that moment the Manx Mouse on the pedestal had its back to him and he had to wait until it completed the revolution and faced him again. To his surprise the reply came, simply and plainly put.

'I'm you—Manxmouse.'

'But you can't be,' protested Manxmouse, 'for there's only one of me. It says so everywhere. I'm the only one in existence.'

Again he had to wait. 'Well, you're not,' said Manxmouse II, 'There are two of us, for here we are. I suppose I'm your other self. Everybody has one, even a Manx Mouse.'

'But I don't understand,' said Manxmouse I, 'What is it like to have two selves? I always thought there was just me.'

Manxmouse II revolved again. He did it quite slowly and almost majestically and he began to speak as soon as his right eye caught Manxmouse I and continued until he had lost sight of him with his left eye, so that he could get in quite a little speech. 'Well, now you know. One of of us is the Manx Mouse that the World sees, rather a calm and noble exterior, friendly and helpful. He never gets flustered. Cool and collected. A friend in need to everyone. An absolutely splendid figure of a Manx Mouse. And the other . . .' Here Manxmouse II's back was turned and Manxmouse I had to wait until he came around again. '. . . . and the other is worried, insecure and is secretly frightened inside himself, especially by things he doesn't understand. He is inclined to want to run away instead of standing up to whatever he must. Also he believes what other people tell him to frighten him.'

'But which one am I?' asked Manxmouse I, now thoroughly confused.

'Look behind you,' said Manxmouse II.

Manxmouse I did so and let out a shriek of terror, 'Help!'

For there, three times larger than Burra Khan had been, eyes bigger than platters and shooting sparks of red fire, mouth open like a cavern showing long, gleaming white fangs, and claws like scimitars unsheathed, tailless hind-quarters wriggling for the pounce, was Manx Cat. This was the end!

'Help! Help!' screamed Manxmouse I, again and in a last dash to escape, ran up the pillar of the pedestal where he cowered next to Manxmouse II who was sitting there quite calmly and undisturbed, as the great, evil-looking beast towered over them prepared to strike and kill.

'H-how did he get in here?' quavered Manxmouse I and closed his eyes because he could not bear to look any more at his doom.

'I didn't bring him,' said Manxmouse II, 'so you must have.'

'M-me?' said Manxmouse I.

'Of course! Who else? And when will you make up your mind which Manx Mouse you really are?'

And then, terrified as he was, Manxmouse I remembered something. He opened his eyes, drew a deep breath and as the pedestal turned around again so that he found himself face to face with the monstrous beast, he stood up on his hind legs and cried, 'I'm not afraid of the biggest

Manx Cat that ever lived! And anyway, I'm on to you! I invented you because I was frightened of Manx Cat. You're nothing but a Clutterbumph!'

At this the apparition of the Manx Cat began to fade and grew dim. Manxmouse heard a snarl and a growl 'Grrr!' and 'Arrgh!' and a voice saying, 'You're sure you're not frightened any more?'

'Absolutely!' replied Manxmouse I. 'Go away!'

The terrible Manx Cat vanished completely. 'Oh dear,' came the voice of the Clutterbumph, 'you're always spoiling my fun! Well, I shall be interested to see how brave you are when you meet the real Manx Cat.' And with a final 'Grrrrrmph!' he flew off.

'That's the boy!' said Manxmouse II. 'You jolly well fixed him.'

'But who and which and what am I, then? Which Manx Mouse?' pleaded Manxmouse I.

'Whichever one you truly want and dare to be,' replied Manxmouse II.

'Then I must go and find Manx Cat, wherever he is and meet him face to face, whatever happens and not be afraid.'

'Good luck, then!' said Manxmouse II and spoke no more. Manxmouse I and his wax replica continued slowly revolving under the spotlights.

He wanted to reflect, but the going round and round on the turntable was making him dizzy. He got down and went away from the room of the Special Attraction and crept along in the semi-darkness, finally sitting down at the feet of one of the figures, not noticing that it was that of Sir Winston Churchill who never in his life had been afraid of anyone or anything. And there Manxmouse thought.

And looking back he remembered that he himself had not been afraid in the long ago, before everyone had told him, 'Look out for Manx Cat!'—'You belong to Manx Cat!'—'Manx Cat is going to eat you!' but after a while it had begun to worry him and cause him to think about it and be frightened.

He had run away from the brown man with the broom and he had run away from the circus, and he had run away from the auction. But actually in truth he had been running away from Manx Cat and this simply would not do. If a meeting with Manx Cat was indeed to be his fate, then instead of trying to avoid it, he must go forward quickly to face it. And as for being eaten by him when he got there, well, that was something else again, and would be decided between Manx Cat and himself.

For even a mouse could fight and perhaps turn the tide of battle. If not, then it was better to finish down Manx Cat's throat, kicking and biting, scratching and struggling than forever to live in fear of the day. He would start off upon what might be his last adventure the very next morning.

And having come to this decision, he found himself feeling extraordinarily peaceful, secure and almost happy and quite exhausted after all the excitement. So, curling up between the feet of Sir Winston, he went off to sleep, not to awaken until half-past eight.

He got up remembering everything that had happened the night before and his decision. He gave his fur a couple of licks to spruce himself up and went off towards the staircase, where as he descended, he saw the policeman standing on the first landing and it seemed to him that he would be as good as anyone to ask where and how to find Manx Cat.

'Please, sir,' he asked, 'could you tell me where I would be able to find Manx Cat?'

'Manx Cat?' replied the policeman, 'Well, now that would be on the Isle of Man, wouldn't it?'

Manxmouse did not find it at all surprising that the policeman replied to his question. But indeed it was most unusual. It was actually the first time in the entire history of Madame Tussaud's Waxworks that he had ever spoken. For to everbody else he wasn't real, only realistic—a wax figure that appeared to be alive. Generations of visitors and tourists as well as children had come up to him and asked, 'Is this the way to the . . .?', or 'Can you tell us where . . .?' and in each case had broken off in mid sentence, laughing at themselves as they realized what fools they had been to be taken in. But to Manxmouse, since it wasn't yet opening time, he had replied most politely.

'The Isle of Man!' Manxmouse repeated, 'But I don't know how to get there. It's very important.'

'To meet Manx Cat?' asked the policeman.

'Yes, to meet Manx Cat.'

'Well now, that's very brave of you,' said the constable. 'First of all then, we'd better have a look and see where it is.'

And with that he pulled a small booklet from one pocket of his tunic in which there seemed to be a map of the British Isles, and consulted it. 'Hmm, let's see now. It doesn't seem to be down at this end. That big one's the Isle of Wight. Now what's this little fellow off here? No, that's not it. That would be Lundy Isle. It wouldn't be in the Scillies. Oh, here we are! Right up in the Irish Sea,' and he leaned down so that Manxmouse could see it on the map himself.

It seemed to be a fair-sized pink blob, sharp at one end and blunt at the other, midway between the North of Ireland and Britain. 'However would I get there?' asked Manxmouse.

The constable traced a line across the sea with his fingernail, 'Why, by boat from Liverpool, I suppose. Well now, you'd be wanting to know about trains and boats, wouldn't you?'

'Yes, please,' said Manxmouse.

The constable put his booklet away and produced another one. He thumbed the pages. 'Liverpool to the Isle of Man——Liverpool——Liverpool,' he mumbled to himself. 'Oh, here we are . . . that would be from Euston Station. There's an eleven o'clock boat train to Liverpool docks that connects with the two-thirty steamer to Douglas on the Isle. Restaurant car on the train. No trouble, the carriages draw right up at the pier and you've no distance to go at all.'

'But how do I get to Euston Station?'

'Oh, Euston!' the constable was on firm ground now. 'The station's only a few minutes from here. Number 30 bus. It goes right by the door.'

'Oh, thank you!' said Manxmouse. 'What time is it now?'

'The time?' said the constable, consulting his wrist-watch, 'The time—why, it's just . . .' But he never finished his sentence, for from the side door below came the rattle of keys and cheery voices saying:

'Hello, Bill!'

'Mornin', Tom!'

'Have a good night, Alf?'

The attendants were letting themselves in preparatory to opening up for the day.

The policeman fell silent and was never heard to speak again. And shortly after a nearby church clock eventually completed his answer for Manxmouse by striking the hour of nine.

At the last stroke of the clock, the doors were thrown open for the day's business. All those who had seen Manxmouse nip inside the night before were waiting with tickets in their hands. With a whoop and a holler they came pouring in shouting, 'The Manx Mouse, the Manx Mouse! Now we'll get him. Where is he?'

So excited were they that they never noticed the little creature who slipped out of the door between their feet.

'Upstairs and to the right for the Manx Mouse,' called the attendants. The mob went trampling up past the silent policeman and hurled itself upon the little figure on the pedestal. People fought each other over him, for they were sure there would be a reward offered. And by the time they discovered he was wax and squashed flat in the struggle.

the real Manx Mouse had escaped again.

For as he reached Marylebone Road and the bus stop, a Number 30 which said 'EUSTON STATION' on it, was just drawing up. An old lady carrying a black shopping bag was waiting to get on. Manxmouse jumped into the bag. Old lady, shopping bag and Manxmouse boarded the bus. The conductor gave two dings on the bell and off they went. There were several stops before the conductor called out, 'Euston! Euston!'

As Manxmouse leapt out of the shopping bag, the bus conductor saw him, gave him a wink and said, 'Good luck with the Manx Cat, chum!'

'Thank you!' said Manxmouse, but didn't even ask or wonder how a strange bus conductor could know about Manx Cat. One thing was certain, he himself was no longer worried.

He hustled across the pavement and into the station, keeping along the side to be well away from the thousands of shuffling feet. It was a very noisy and confusing place and the first railway station he had ever visited. So with an hour and a half to spare, he inspected all its exciting booths, shops, newspaper kiosks and ticket offices. He watched porters rushing about trundling baggage. The hiss of steam and the shrieks of impatient locomotives were thrilling. And once he had got to the place from which the trains actually departed, there were no further problems for they were all listed on boards at the side of the entrance gates. After a few moments of search and inspection, Manxmouse came across the one that said, '11.00 LIVERPOOL EXPRESS Connecting with S.S. MANXBELLE.'

He had no trouble getting past the ticket inspector. True, the press and Mr Smeater were still combing London, poking into every likely place where a Manx Mouse might possibly be, but actually they were the only ones.

For it was another day and the Million-Pound Manx Mouse was only a twenty-four-hour sensation. What London was now interested in was a new pop singer who had arrived from America wearing his jacket on his legs, his trousers over his head, his hair in plastic curlers and whose speciality was singing 'O Sole Mio' with a large portion of codfish cakes in his mouth.

But since Manxmouse had committed no crime, no police alert had gone out to watch all railway stations, airports or piers. And so he simply marched through, walking under the suitcase carried by a commercial traveller going north, onto the platform. There he popped into the guard's compartment of the train, certain that while the guard would be going through the carriages asking everybody for tickets, he surely would not be looking for anyone in his own cubbyhole.

At eleven o'clock exactly, the platform guard waved a flag and blew a whistle, doors thunked shut, the engine shrieked and gave a clang or two, there was a jolt and crashing of bumpers and the Liverpool-Isle of Man Express and Manxmouse were on their way.

12

The Story of Manxmouse meets Manx Cat

THE train ride to Liverpool was uneventful. Manxmouse would very much have liked to have gone up to see what the restaurant car was like, for he had had no breakfast and as lunchtime approached, grew hungrier and hungrier. However, this did not matter for at noon the guard obligingly opened his box lunch, thoughtfully provided by his wife, which contained a veal and ham pie with a piece of egg in the middle, some cake and a flask of tea. But since the train swayed, shook and joggled, Manxmouse was able to join him at his meal from the quite adequate amount of crumbs that fell to the floor.

Fortunately when they reached Liverpool the guard remained away and Manxmouse, climbing up onto a shelf, was able to observe the fascinating ride down the waterfront, past the dozens of great docks. There, ships of every kind, size and colour from all parts of the world, flying their flags, were surrounded by a veritable forest of cranes.

It was, of course, cold and raining in Liverpool. A fair-sized steamer, The *Manxbelle*, lay alongside the Prince's Stage landing. The train doors were opened and all the passengers flowed from their carriages across the dock, up the gangplank and into the ship. When the guard came to fetch his overcoat and tin lunch box from his compartment, Manxmouse jumped down and joined the throng. The guard turned and stared for a moment as though he had seen something and then decided he had not. By that time Manxmouse was aboard.

The departure, too, was exciting and noisy, with the ship blowing its siren. Bells clanged, sailors shouted and the vessel shuddered as its engines turned and it began to move away from the pier.

Manxmouse watched the departure from under the rail, until they were out of sight of land. Since there was nothing more to do or see and it was both wet and chilly, he decided to go inside the main lounge and warm himself, until something more interesting turned up.

And here he had a most extraordinary stroke of luck. For a passenger had fallen asleep and one of those pamphlets that are always being put out by steamship companies, railways or tourist offices, had slipped through his fingers to the floor. It most conveniently fell right at the feet of Manxmouse. Entitled *Welcome to the Isle of Man*, it was full of the most fascinating facts about his destination, all of which he felt could in some way or another be highly useful to him in his forthcoming encounter with Manx Cat.

He read: 'The Island, known to the Romans as *Mona*, is about 33 miles long and 12 miles broad, containing much beautiful scenery, often of the rugged type, as well as a fine seaboard. It is lozenge-shaped with *Snaefell*, 2,034 feet, its highest point and reached by a mountain railway. Its capital is Douglas. There are many splendid beaches, holiday resorts and ancient ruins. The climate is mild.

'There are no snakes or toads, no badgers, foxes, moles, voles or squirrels on the Island. The pigmy shrew is abundant, as is the long-tailed field mouse (*Mus sylvaticus*) and the house mouse, too, is well established.

'Excellent!' Manxmouse mused, 'No other enemies and plenty of friends.'

But now he came upon the most exciting piece of information:

'The Manx Cat without a tail, or with a greatly reduced tail, is common as a domestic pet in the Island. Whether the tailless cat reached the Isle of Man from elsewhere, or whether it developed there is not known. The fur is usually longer and more lax than in ordinary cats. They may be of any colour and the cat has what is termed a double coat, namely soft and open, with a thick under-coat. Its rump is as round as an orange and its hind-quarters high, which is what gives it a rabbity or hopping gait, and in some places they are even known as rabbit cats. Many people suppose they are part rabbit, even though this is impossible.'

Manxmouse was fascinated. 'Why, if they were,' he said to himself, 'we'd be relatives, because of my rabbit ears.'

He read on.

'The Manx Cat or "Rumpy", is one of the mysteries of the feline race and at the same time one of the most interesting and unusual of all the cats. Lively, extremely brave, a patient and skilful hunter, it is an affectionate companion with a cry differing from that of other members of the species. They are very intelligent. No two accounts agree on their origin. There are various stories of the first one having arrived on a trading vessel from the Far East, where tailless cats are more common. Another tells of how one of the ships of the Spanish Armada was wrecked on Spanish Rock, close to the Island and that some tailless cats swam ashore. The third possibility is that they began right on the Isle of Man.'

Manxmouse read it all with the greatest of interest, absorbing further information about this strange island divided down the middle, north and south, by a range of mountains; its past history when it was ruled by kings and queens; its other towns where there were many ancient and prehistoric sites, plus the fact that it was the setting of a famous annual motorcycle race.

By the time he had finished there was a hooting and clanging of bells and backward churning of engines, and then a bump. They had arrived! He waited until all the passengers had gone ashore and then scampered down the gangplank, through the waiting room, out of the pier into Douglas High Street, and thence from the town, leaving the sea behind him.

The rain stopped and the sun came out as Manxmouse set off towards the interior. He had gone only a short distance when he saw a chicken striding towards him, her head in the air. Manxmouse could not help staring. The chicken halted and said severely, 'Young fellow, just what are you gawking at?'

Manxmouse replied, 'Excuse me, I didn't mean to but I couldn't help it. You haven't a tail.'

'Well, neither have you,' said the chicken.

'But I'm a Manx Mouse.'

'Well, I'm a Manx Fowl.'

'Have all the chick . . . er . . . I mean . . . er . . . fowls on the Island no tails?' asked Manxmouse.

'Only us aristocrats,' said the Manx Fowl loftily, 'there are plenty of common ones.'

'And are there any other animals on the Island that have no tails?' Manxmouse asked, for there had been nothing in the pamphlet about the Manx Fowl.

'No,' said the bird, 'only us. Unless you want to count those cats. But they're pretty common and quite absurd-looking. To us it's becoming.'

'But it's the Manx Cat I'm looking for,' said Manxmouse. 'Can you tell me where I could find him?'

'Is it the one that's expecting you?' asked the Manx Fowl.

'Oh,' said Manxmouse, 'I'm expected, am I?' and it came as something of a shock to him. He had hoped to be able to walk up to Manx Cat as a surprise and rather take him off his guard.

'Of course,' said the Manx Fowl. 'Straight down this road there's a lane leading off to the right, and it's the first house you come to. You can't miss it,' and the Manx Fowl stalked off.

Manxmouse could not help feeling that in spite of her superiority, she too, looked pretty silly without a tail.

The house was there, a small modest cottage with a thatched roof and the whitewashed walls nicely beamed in the old style. As he approached, Manx Cat came out of the door and looking down the road waved to him and said, 'This way. Here we are. Welcome! A bit late, aren't you?'

'Am I?' said Manxmouse, 'I'm sorry.'

Manx Cat came forward, his paw outstretched to greet him. He was a fine-looking, sturdy animal, tiger-striped like a tabby but with markings around his eyes that gave him the effect of peering through spectacles. Manxmouse noticed that he was somewhat hippy, in fact round as a butter ball at his hind and tailless end.

'Thomas R. Manx Cat is the name,' he said. 'But just call me Tom.'

'I'm Manxmouse—Harrison G.'

'Delighted to see you Harrison, old boy.'

'How do you do?' said Manxmouse. They shook hands.

It was all so completely different from what Manxmouse had expected and steeled himself for, so that he hardly knew what to say or do. For there was nothing at all fierce or terrifying about Manx Cat. True, he was a big, powerful specimen but the spectacle markings around his eyes gave him an unexpected air of benevolence.

He was, of course, huge compared to Manxmouse and could have swallowed him at one gulp, but there seemed to be no inclination in him to do so. He had splendid amber-coloured eyes and a proud spread of whiskers. It was he who broke the silence. 'Had a good crossing?'

'Not too bad,' replied Manxmouse.

'Lucky for some. The Irish Sea at this time of year can kick up very nasty. Did you lunch on the boat?'

'As a matter of fact I didn't,' said Manxmouse.

'Well then, you'll be wanting a cup of tea. Come in and meet the wife. She'll be getting it ready.'

Manxmouse followed. It was slightly disorganizing, to say the least, to have come prepared for battle and be invited in to tea instead.

And what a pleasant tea, in a charming little dining-room with a table set out with a tea cloth, excellent china, with crocheted doilys, plates of sandwiches, scones, toasted muffins, biscuits and other treats.

A sweet-faced Manx tabby with a white blaze on her throat came forward to greet them. 'My wife Margery,' said Manx Cat. 'This is Harrison G. Manxmouse. He didn't lunch on the boat and is about ready for a good tuck-in.'

'Do come in,' Margery Manx Cat said, 'We're delighted to see you. Tom would have been so disappointed if you hadn't come. He's been looking forward to meeting you for ages.'

In a corner there were three kittens in a basket. One had no tail at all; the second just a trace of a stumpy one and the third a quite normal appendage. They all shouted, 'Tea! Tea, Mummy! Can we have tea, too?'

'Not now, darlings, later,' their mother replied, and then said to Manxmouse, who was looking at them admiringly, 'Children! They are all alike, aren't they? We are a little upset about the one with a tail. He's going to feel it dreadfully later on in life. But that's one of our problems, we never know what we're going to produce. In my last litter all of them were tailless. I can tell you we were very proud. Won't you sit down?'

'Yes, yes, old boy,' urged Tom, 'make yourself at home.

It's good to see you.'

The three sat around the table. Margery poured and was most hospitable and solicitous, offering mustard and cress sandwiches and hot-buttered muffins with strawberry jam, as well as little coloured, iced cakes which were delicious and had some kind of a fruity filling. Manxmouse, who as usual was hungry, did not hold back and thoroughly enjoyed the meal.

'There's nothing like travelling to give one an appetite,' Tom Manx Cat said, not backward himself at tucking into the buttered scones. 'I see you like those chocolate biscuits. Do have another, since they're the last you'll ever be eating, Harrison old fellow.'

Manxmouse looked up into Manx Cat's face to see whether he had heard aright. But he seemed not to have noticed that he had said anything untoward, and was looking even more benevolent as he handed the plate of chocolate-covered wafers to Manxmouse, merely remarking, 'The Doom, you know.'

Manxmouse did not know, and the word had not a nice sound. He probably had mistaken Manx Cat's meaning.

'Tea now! Tea now, Mummy!' cried the kittens, seeing that the grown-ups had about finished. 'And then may Mr Harrison Manxmouse play with us?'

'Very well, then,' their mother replied, 'you may all have your tea now. But you mustn't bother our guest,' and then to Manxmouse, 'Shall we go into the drawing-room where we can chat quietly?' As they passed through the door she looked back at her kittens and remarked, 'They're such a joy to me.'

'They're adorable,' said Manxmouse and forgot the momentary shadow that had been cast over him at the tea table. He thought only of how kind and hospitable Tom Manx Cat was and what a delightful person and good mother was his wife Margery.

The drawing-room was nicely decorated and gay with chintzes and comfortable furniture. Tom motioned Manxmouse to an easy chair, took another himself as his wife curled herself up on the couch. 'Smoke?' he asked.

'No, thank you,' said Manxmouse.

'We've never formed the habit either. Were you able to have a sleep on the way over?'

'No,' replied Manxmouse. 'Actually I became too interested in reading all about—ah—you people, and how you were supposed to have come here when a ship of the Spanish Armada was wrecked . . .'

'Ho!' snorted Tom Manx Cat while his wife smiled indulgently, 'That old chestnut! Such a lot of nonsense. We couldn't have landed here from the wreck of a Spanish galleon, for the simple reason that there have never been any tailless cats in Spain. The real story goes back a lot farther than the Armada, to the time of the Flood and Noah's Ark, when the animals went in two by two. Did you know that the cat was the last of all to go aboard?'

'No,' said Manxmouse, 'I didn't. Why was that?'

'Well,' said Tom, 'the way it was told to me by my grandfather, the cat wouldn't go into the Ark without taking a mouse with it. The mouse was being difficult, for it wasn't quite certain what the cat had in mind—whether it was being invited to join the cruise out of politeness, or to guarantee a continuation in the supply of mice. I must say,' Manx Cat commented at this point, 'one is able to see the situation from the mouse's point of view: stay behind and drown, or go along and be eaten. Not much of a choice, eh, friend Harrison?'

'Tom!' said Margery Manx Cat warningly.

Tom Manx Cat coughed somewhat delicately and said quickly, 'What I was coming to was the point of the story, namely that with all the animals nicely inside and the rain starting to come down, old Noah lost his patience and slammed the door just as the cat squeezed through at the last moment, and cut off her tail. On the way to Mount Ararat, Noah stopped here to take on water . . .'

'Water?' queried Manxmouse.

'Well, something,' Manx Cat said. 'There's supposed

173

to be a stone down by the shore marking the spot where he landed. Anyway, he opened the door. Last on, first off! That was my ancestor and we've been here without tails ever since. Now tell us something about yourself.'

Manxmouse replied, 'Oh, I've had all manner of strange things happen to me,' and recounted one or two of them and then added, 'but they all ended up with everyone saying that I belong to Manx Cat and feeling rather sorry for me. I never quite understood.'

Manx Cat nodded and said, 'Yes, of course, that would be the Doom. The word would get around.'

His wife Margery suddenly looked distressed and murmured, 'Oh, that dreadful Doom.'

'What word would get around?' Manxmouse said.

'Why, naturally, that I'm to eat you,' Tom replied coolly. 'But officially, of course, in a little while and according to the regulations, in front of proper witnesses, as per Section 2, paragraph 3 of the Doom.'

'But what *is* a Doom?' Manxmouse asked uncomfortably. It was one thing for him to be prepared to face up to Manx Cat and quite another to be made welcome, disarmed by being given a high tea and then hearing his end quite calmly discussed, all beautifully organized and arranged beforehand.

'A Doom,' explained Tom patiently, 'is something written down on an old piece of parchment by someone, usually a witch or a wizard, a long, long time ago. It tells what is going to happen to the person upon whom the Doom is pronounced. And it always does. You can't escape a Doom, you know. Yours was washed up in a casket out of the sea. At least, half of it was, the half that matters. Shall I get it for you? You might like to have a look at it yourself.'

'Yes, please, I should like to very much,' said Manxmouse. He was not meaning at all to be sarcastic; he really was interested, since it seemed to concern him.

'Would you fetch it, my dear?' said Tom. Margery arose and went to a cupboard from whence she took a weathered casket of oak, bound in brass and studded with iron nails. In it was a rolled up parchment with faded writing upon it.

Tom Manx Cat studied it for a moment and the spectacle markings around his eyes made him look like a professor about to give a lecture. His lips moved as he read silently and then said, 'The first part is a bit long—it's all about the wars between the Manx Cats and the Manx Mice, thousands of years ago. History was never my favourite subject, but it seems in the early days the Manx Mice outnumbered the Manx Cats. But afterwards we won and drove them all into the sea.' He unrolled more of the manuscript and then said, 'Oh, here we come to the interesting part: ". . . and it came to pass that one Manx Mouse did escape and on the Third Day of May, a thousand years hence, shall return to the Isle of Man with the Doom upon him."'

Here Tom Manx Cat looked up and said, 'You see how beautifully a Doom works out? That's today.'

'Yes, I do see,' said Manxmouse.

Manx Cat continued, '"And he shall be greeted by Manx Cat with courtesy and politeness, offered a meal and thereafter be led out to the execution grounds before properly assembled witnesses and, in accordance with the

175

regulations for the procedure, be swallowed by Manx Cat, thus carrying out the conditions as herein set forth. The regulations for the manner of the execution shall be as follows . . ." ' And here the parchment came to an end for it had been torn in half and the other portion seemed to be missing.

'What did the rest of it say?' Manxmouse asked.

'Well, we haven't got that part,' said Tom, 'but it really doesn't matter, because we know how it's done. It's been handed down. You bow to me; I bow to you. I pounce and swallow and it's all over. I promise you, you won't feel a thing. Besides . . .'

'Oh, Tom!' Margery interrupted, 'Must we really? I've seen Blue Persians, Blue Seal Siamese, North Holland Blue Hens, Blue Tits, Blue Jays, Blue Fish, but never a Blue Mouse. Are you *sure* he's a Manx Mouse? *The* Manx Mouse, I mean?'

Tom said, 'You will have observed, of course my dear, that he has no tail? Pure Manx strain.'

'But those ears of his . . .' Margery insisted, for she found that she had unexpectedly become fond of him, '. . . like a rabbit; and our hippety-hop hind legs. Supposing we were related?—And besides, the kittens seem to like him. He could stay here with us and play with them.'

Tom Manx Cat sighed, rolled up the parchment and replaced it in the box. 'I agree, it's a pity,' he said, and then smiled genially at Manxmouse adding, 'I've taken rather a fancy to you myself, and would enjoy knowing you better. But then, there is the Doom,' and here he tapped the box. 'What can anyone do about it? And—ah . . . ah . . .', here he glanced at his watch, 'it's set for six o'clock, I'm afraid. It's just a quarter to, now.'

'Where is it to take place?' Manxmouse asked.

'Well, you know how it is,' Tom replied, 'you mean to ask only a few people and then you find that there are more and more you can't leave out. So I've arranged for it in the stadium. It's just a few minutes from here, over the hill. Would you like to say goodbye to the kittens?'

'Yes, I would,' said Manxmouse. 'They're so sweet.' Something had happened to him so that to all intents and purposes, he had given up. For there was the document in the casket with, as Manx Cat had pointed out, even the proper day. All the details seemed to have been organized so smoothly and Tom Manx Cat was so convinced that it was right, that Manxmouse no longer even thought of escaping. If a wizard had written it all down on an old parchment, then there was not any use in trying to run away.

They went into the other room where the kittens left off stuffing themselves with what remained of the tea and crowded around Manxmouse crying, 'Must you go? Please stay here and play with us. We like you!'

Manxmouse said goodbye to each one and even spoke

177

words of encouragement to the kitten with the tail, telling him that in the outside world away from the Island, there were millions upon millions of cats, all of them had tails and he really would not mind having one when he got used to it.

Tom Manx Cat coughed discreetly and said, 'It's five minutes to six. We ought to start,' and then to his wife, 'Coming, darling?'

At which Margery suddenly burst into tears and cried, 'No, I'm not! I think your old Doom is horrid! I don't want it to happen! And if you were half a Manx Cat, you wouldn't go either.'

Tom Manx Cat looked rather uneasy, as males do in the face of a feminine storm. He said, 'Look here, darling, I don't like the idea any better than you do. I'm not hungry to begin with; I haven't eaten a mouse in years. I like this little fellow too, but when there's a Doom, you've got to . . .'

'Oh, go away, you and your old Doom!' Margery sobbed and gathered up her kittens to her, who all began to cry as well.

'I think we'd best be on our way,' Tom Manx Cat said.

'Yes,' said Manxmouse, 'we'd better go.'

Manx Cat had spoken truly, for it was indeed no more

than a few minutes walk over the brow of the hill. As they topped it, they saw the stadium down in the hollow, oval-shaped and with a number of entrances. At one stood a Manx Cat attendant who saluted as they drew near and a clock struck six. 'Right on time!' said the attendant. 'Have you the Doom?'

'Here, under my arm,' said Manx Cat, indicating the casket. 'Have all the witnesses arrived?'

'All here and assembled,' replied the attendant, 'I'll lead the way in.' He walked before them down a narrow passageway leading to the field which at that time happened to be laid out for football.

The seats rose in banked tiers and there the witnesses were seated and waiting. And as Manxmouse saw them, he got the surprise of his life. For there were all the people he had met during the strange adventures that had formed the greater part of his brief life.

There was Billibird, his tail light flashing on and off, sitting next to House Cat Mother who was chatting to old One-Eye.

A whole section of the grandstand was given over to the Clutterbumphs, dozens of them. There were every body's Clutterbumphs in all their various guises—witch, ghost and bogey Clutterbumphs, devil ones, monster,

spider, dragon, snake and burglar Clutterbumphs, the lot.

They were there in a holiday mood, yelling, grrrumphing, screaming, shouting and laughing with one another.

When Manxmouse entered, they all pointed at him and shrieked, 'There he is, the little brute! That's the one who's been spoiling all our fun! Now we shall have some of our own back!'

The frog was there and Captain Hawk and the fox with the entire Bumbleton pack sitting next to him, and Squire Ffuffer with Miss Blenkinsop. Nelly was so enormous that she occupied a whole section to herself with Burra Khan close by.

Manxmouse recognized Mr Smeater, the pet shop owner, the taxi-driver and the policeman from Madame Tussaud's who had given him the directions how to get to the Isle of Man. And in the front row Wendy and Mr Mellow were sitting together. Wendy looked as though she had been crying and Mr Mellow had his arm about her. The lorry driver was there too. Other parts of the stands were taken up with hundreds upon hundreds of Manx Cats, Manx Fowls, pigmy shrews, long-tailed field mice, house mice and other animals to be found on the Island.

As they walked across the field a hush fell upon the assemblage. The policeman climbed down out of the stands and came over to meet them.

'He's going to referee,' said Tom. 'And see there's fair play.'

'What do you mean, fair play?' Manxmouse asked. 'I thought you just pounce and swallow.'

'Well, to see that I do it properly and in accordance with the regulations,' Manx Cat said. 'So now I'll say goodbye, for you go over there and I go over here until we're called and——er . . . might we shake hands? For you do know I'm sorry, don't you? I think you're being a jolly good sport about it all.'

They shook hands and Manxmouse said, 'You've been very kind, too. And thank you for the tea.'

Manx Cat retired to one side of the field, while Manxmouse went to the other. The policeman, who had taken the casket, stood in the centre. He removed his helmet, wiped his brow with a handkerchief, took the scroll out and began to read its contents to the spectators.

When he came to the part of the Doom that was upon Manxmouse and how it was about to be carried out, Wendy cried, 'But I don't want anyone to hurt him!'

Mr Mellow said, 'Hush! Never despair!'

Mr Smeater rose in his seat shouting, 'He's my Manx Mouse! You can't do this to him! He's worth a million pounds!'

Two Manx Cats pulled him down and put their paws over his mouth.

The taxi-driver said, 'Coo! And I 'ad 'im in me cab all the time.'

The lorry driver looked around at Mr Smeater and growled, 'Five bob 'e give me for 'im!'

Having finished his reading the policeman returned the parchment to the box, set it upon the ground and motioning with his left and his right hand, said, 'Will the two parties please come to the centre now and carry out the Doom.'

As Manxmouse and Manx Cat approached one another from the opposite ends of the arena, the word 'Doom' seemed to cast its spell upon everyone present. Even Mr Mellow was looking nervous and worried and as for Wendy, large tears were falling from her eyes. But nobody moved or spoke.

The policeman announced, 'You've all heard the Doom. The rules are as follows: Manxmouse! When I drop my hat, that will be the signal. You will advance three paces, bow to Manx Cat and remain standing. You may close your eyes then, if you like. Manx Cat! Upon observance of same signal, you will advance three paces, bow to Manxmouse and prepare to pounce and swallow. You are allowed three preliminary waggles. Now remember, there's to be no torture; no play; no tossing of him up into the air and catching of him; no teasing or bashing him about. Three waggles, a pounce, a nice clean swallow and Bob's your uncle.'

The policeman stepped back a little so as to be out of the way and held up his helmet. In solemn tones he asked, 'Are you ready, Manxmouse?'

'Yes, quite,' came the reply and so quiet was it in the stadium that you could hear his tiny voice perfectly, right up into the last row.

'Ready, Manx Cat?'

'Ready!'

'Then GO!' and the policeman dropped his hat.

Manxmouse took three paces forward and dutifully bowed.

Manx Cat did the same.

Manx Cat gave two waggles and then stopped the third halfway through in utter astonishment.

For Manxmouse not only had not closed his eyes, but he was standing up on his kangaroo hind legs, his left paw extended in front of him, his right one cocked and his tiny white teeth bared. 'Come on, then!' he cried, 'And let's see if you can swallow me!'

He had had enough of it all: the nonsense about the Doom and everyone taking it for granted that because of some silly words written down a thousand years ago he,

Manxmouse, would today quietly march down the throat of Manx Cat. He had come there determined to meet whatever fate had in store for him, but meeting it did not mean to submit to it by any means. He had made up his mind the night before in Madame Tussaud's that he would fight.

Somehow they had almost talked him out of his determination, what with all that silly business of the Doom that could not be escaped and a half-torn piece of parchment in an old box. Talk! Talk! Old wives' tales and threats! No wonder the world was full of Clutterbumphs, if one believed all the nonsense people poured into one's ears. Besides, as his image had inquired of him in the Waxworks' Museum, which Manxmouse was he: the one who had been taught fear so that sometimes he had run away? Or the absolutely splendid figure of a Manxmouse who had said, '. . . I must go and find Manx Cat wherever he is, and meet him face to face and whatever happens, not be afraid.'?

Well, he knew now which Manxmouse he was. He was no longer to be frightened by things real or imaginary. If he went down anyone's throat it would be while battling with might and main.

Manx Cat, then, stopped in mid waggle and said, 'What's this? You're going to fight?'

'Yes,' said Manxmouse, 'I am. Come on, then, and let's get on with it,' and he took half a step forward.

Manx Cat took half a step backwards and looked over towards the policeman. 'He says he's going to fight. But that's ridiculous! In the first place mice don't fight and in the second, it's against the Doom.'

'I don't care what your old Doom says,' Manxmouse declared, 'I'm not giving up. Are you ready?' And this time he took a full step forward.

Manx Cat made a full leap backwards. 'Oh, look here now . . .' he began, when he was drowned out by the chorus of cheers and shouts and cries of encouragement from the stands.

'Oh, Manxmouse, you're wonderful!' Wendy cried.

184

'Bully for you, Manxmouse!' shouted Mr Mellow. 'Lead with your left!'

All the Clutterbumphs fell silent and looked at one another in astonishment and confusion, mumbling, 'He's not afraid! He's still not afraid! We were sure he would be. This is no place for us,' and Grumphing, Whooing and Arghing, they arose as one to leave.

Nelly the Nellyphant took up the refrain, 'That's right! He's not afraid of Manx Cat and I'm not afraid of Manxmouse! That means I'm not afraid of anything any more. Shall I come down and step on him for you?'

'I'll give you air cover and dive-bomb him,' shrieked Captain Hawk, flapping his wings and preparing to take off.

Squire Ffuffer, quite red in the face, arose and said, 'Let me set the Bumbleton pack onto him!'

General Hound bayed, 'A cat-chase boys. Oh, I say, what fun that would be!'

Joe Reynard yipped, 'I'll nip that fat bottom of his for him.'

Mr Smeater admonished, 'For heaven's sakes be careful! Remember you're worth a million pounds! Don't get yourself hurt.'

But the taxi-driver encouraged, 'Stout fella! Why, Manx Cat's nothing but an old alley cat with no tail! I'll give 'im the toe of me boot and that'll be the end of 'im!'

Burra Khan growled, 'If it comes to swallowing, let me do some. I eat Manx Cats as appetizers.'

'No, no,' cried Manxmouse. 'I don't want any help. I don't need any. This is my fight and I'm ready to carry on alone.' And here with his left well extended, as Mr

Mellow had advised, he began making little leaping movements back and forth to warm up while with his right paw he kept bumping his nose to get his muscles limbered to let fly.

But instead of putting up his own guard, or waggling any more, Manx Cat sat down and looked helplessly at the policeman. 'Well, here's a fine how-do-you-do,' he said. 'What do we do now?' His spectacle markings gave him an air of pathetic bewilderment.

The stands were in an uproar, the Manx Cats shouting to their champion to go in and fight; the mice and the other animals cheering Manxmouse. The Clutterbumphs were still departing, squawking, yelling and snarling in utter confusion. Manxmouse's friends were calling advice to him such as:

'Stay away from his right!'

'Keep jabbing!'

'In the body! Manx Cats can't take it down there!'

'Go it Manxmouse!'

The commotion was tremendous.

But eventually, since Manx Cat just sat there looking confused and one couldn't fight with

oneself, Manxmouse had to cease his aggressive movements. And so he also sat down to see what would happen next.

The policeman raised both arms and shouted for quiet and once more a hush fell upon the throng. Manx Cat said unhappily to him, 'What are we to do? Maybe there's something in the last half of the Doom to cover this situation, but we haven't got it.' And he added in an injured tone, 'How am I supposed to pounce and swallow neatly when he keeps jumping about like that?'

The policeman, ignoring him, now turned to Manxmouse and asked, 'Manxmouse, answer me truthfully. Do you really intend to fight Manx Cat?'

'Yes, I do.'

'You're not bluffing?'

'Just you see if I'm bluffing!' said Manxmouse,

baring his teeth and resuming his fighting stance.

The crowd began to make a noise again, when the policeman held up his hands and shouted, 'Quiet! Quiet, please! Ladies and gentlemen, hear me now. I have questioned Manxmouse and he's determined to fight. It just so happens that I have with me the other half of the Doom, which includes the regulations. The manuscript was deposited with us at Tussaud's as a curiosity many years ago.' He reached inside his tunic and withdrew the other half of the torn piece of parchment. 'I'll now read it:

'Section 2, Paragraph 1, regulating the conduct of the Doom. "But if aforesaid Manxmouse instead of yielding and being swallowed shall take a stand in his defence and bravely and gallantly show that he means to fight for his life, then the Doom shall become inoperative, null and void and cancelled. Manxmouse and Manx Cat shall live in peace forever after. And furthermore . . ."'

But whatever the furthermore might have been was never heard, for it was drowned out in the roar of approval and the next moment Manx Cat had his arms about Manxmouse's shoulders and was hugging him and saying, 'Bully for you, old fellow! I couldn't be more pleased and delighted. You know, I was against the whole business from the beginning.'

All Manxmouse's friends then came pouring down out of the grandstand, laughing and crying, trying to pat both Manxmouse and Manx Cat on the back, shaking hands with the policeman, congratulating one another and calling for three cheers for both parties. Such a highly-charged and wonderfully emotional moment had not been seen in the Isle of Man stadium since it had been built.

And that was the way it all ended, with the band playing and Squire Ffuffer, Joe Reynard, Miss Blenkinsop and the entire Bumbleton pack leading a triumphant snake dance with Nelly trumpeting, Burra Khan roaring and Captain Hawk wheeling in circles, screeching congratulations from the sky.

Wendy picked up Manxmouse and held him to her cheek for a moment, saying, 'You're the most wonderful Harrison G. Manxmouse in the whole world!'

But Mr Mellow also shook hands with Manx Cat and said, 'Congratulations, sir, you showed admirable restraint in a difficult situation.'

Manx Cat was almost pathetically pleased to have someone feel that he, too, had done well. 'Do you think so?' he said. 'You see, I'm actually rather fond of the little fellow.'

'So are we all,' said Mr Mellow.

Wendy had given Manxmouse a farewell kiss and set him down again when Mr Smeater rushed up to seize him and try to claim his million pounds. But before he could lay a finger upon Manxmouse, the lorry driver caught up with him.

'Give me five bob for a h'annermul worth a million quid, would yer? Well then, take this!' and drawing back his fist he aimed, and let fly a blow at Mr Smeater's head, which fortunately wasn't there to receive it. For, seeing the lorry driver, he turned and ran for his life.

Around and around the stadium the procession wound and it seemed as though the cheering would never stop, until the policeman went to the centre, waved his helmet, blew his whistle and shouted, 'It's all over, folks! And

Manxmouse belongs to Manx Cat as everybody said he would, but as a friend. We'd better be getting back home now. This way! The last boat leaves in half an hour.'

Still snake dancing, Squire Ffuffer and the procession followed the band out of the stadium. As the music and the cheering died away in the distance, Manxmouse and Manx Cat were left there alone.

'No hard feelings?' Manx Cat asked, somewhat anxiously, for he had not forgotten what he had been proposing to do to Manxmouse.

'Oh no, none at all!' Manxmouse replied generously.

'Splendid!' Tom said, 'Come on, old boy, let's get back to the house, then. I can hardly wait to tell Margery. And won't the kittens be pleased!' He linked his arm with that of Manxmouse and they started home together.

'Shall I confess something to you?' said Manx Cat. 'From the very first moment I saw you, I felt that I would like to have you for a friend.'

'Me too,' said Manxmouse, and felt happier than ever he had before in his life.

As they approached the house, Margery emerged still holding her tear-stained apron to her eyes. But her sadness turned to joy and she gave a cry of delight when she saw them. 'Manxmouse! Oh Tom, you didn't swallow him! I shall always love you for that. What happened?'

So, of course, the story had to be retold, and the kittens came tumbling out of the house shouting and screaming that now Manxmouse could stay and play with them. Both Tom and Margery Manx Cat would hear of nothing else but that Manxmouse must lodge with them until he was able to settle down on his own.

There is little more to recount. Manxmouse remained with Tom and Margery on the Isle of Man until he married a charming little grey, long-tailed field mouse and they built a house quite close to that of the Manx Cat family. Nor was Manxmouse at all surprised when in his wife's first litter, two of the mice had no tails at all and were blue-grey; three had stumps and were pinkish; and four had long tails, were rather orange-coloured and had slightly rabbity ears. For, as Margery Manx Cat had explained, that was the way things sometimes went.

And back in Buntingdowndale, the ceramist never did find out what had happened to the little china mouse he had made that had gone wrong, and which had so mysteriously disappeared from his bedside table.

Piccolo fiction

Keith Chatfield
Issi Noho 35p
Issi Pandemonium 35p

Two books about Issi Noho the panda. He can work a little magic
but, because he can't count too well, his spells always go wrong,
and that's how he comes to Coppins Wood and meets the Martin
family.

Based on the Thames Television series.

Alison Uttley
The Brown Mouse Book 35p

In a hole in a bank, underneath a wild rose bush, live two tiny
field mice, Serena and Snug, who sit out in the sun on fine days
with all the other field mice. All the woodland animals know the
spot as the Rose and Crown, where they drink dandelion tea and
cowslip wine from acorn mugs, and smoke clay pipes of mouse
baccy! This is the lovely setting for five exciting adventures of
Snug and Serena: they meet a queen, Snug is carried off by a
hawk, and Serena has a narrow escape from a weasel.